"That ranch you own? It's worth exactly what you paid for it," Jake said. "Unless, of course, you put a higher price on what you gave old Charlie than those services were truly worth—"

Addison slapped his face.

Hard.

The imprint of her hand stood out on his cheek in crimson relief. His dumbfounded expression told her she'd just scored a perfect shot.

Why hang around and ruin it?

Addison turned her back and faced the crowd.

"Move," she said, and a path opened like the parting of the Red Sea.

She stomped down that path...and stopped, halfway to the front door. *What the hell,* she thought, and she turned to face him one last time.

"You're also a nasty, egotistical, despicable jerk."

The crowd gasped again, then erupted in a frantic buzz of delighted whispers.

She'd given Wilde's Crossing enough to talk about for the next decade.

Wilde by name, unashamedly wild by nature!

They work hard, but you can be damned sure
they play even harder!

For as long as any of them could remember,
they'd always loved the same things:

danger...and beautiful women.

They gladly took up the call to serve their country but *duty, honor* and *pride* are words that mask the scars of a true warrior. Now, one by one, the brothers return to their family ranch in Texas.

Can their hearts be tamed in the place they
once called home?

Meet the deliciously sexy Wilde Brothers in this sizzling and utterly unmissable new family dynasty by much-loved author Sandra Marton!

Look out for Caleb's story next month and Travis's story later in 2013!

Sandra Marton

THE DANGEROUS JACOB WILDE

Recycling programs
for this product may
not exist in your area.

ISBN-13: 978-0-373-23873-6

THE DANGEROUS JACOB WILDE

This edition published by arrangement with Harlequin Books S.A.

For questions and comments about the quality of this book, please contact us at CustomerService@Harlequin.com.

www.Harlequin.com

Printed in U.S.A.

All about the author...
Sandra Marton

SANDRA MARTON wrote her first novel while she was still in elementary school. Her doting parents told her she'd be a writer someday and Sandra believed them. In high school and college, she wrote dark poetry nobody but her boyfriend understood, though looking back, she suspects he was just being kind. As a wife and mother, she wrote murky short stories in what little spare time she could manage, but not even her boyfriend-turned-husband could pretend to understand those. Sandra tried her hand at other things, among them teaching and serving on the board of education in her hometown, but the dream of becoming a writer was always in her heart.

At last Sandra realized she wanted to write books about what all women hope to find: love with that one special man, love that's rich with fire and passion, love that lasts forever. She wrote a novel, her very first, and sold it to Harlequin® Presents. Since then, she's written more than seventy books, all of them featuring sexy, gorgeous, larger-than-life heroes. A four-time RITA® Award finalist, she's also received eight *RT Book Reviews* awards for Best Harlequin® Presents of the Year and has been honored with an *RT Book Reviews* Career Achievement Award for Series Romance. Sandra lives with her very own sexy, gorgeous, larger-than-life hero in a sun-filled house on a quiet country lane in the northeastern United States.

Sandra loves to hear from her readers. You can contact her through her website, www.sandramarton.com, **or at P.O. Box 295, Storrs CT 06268.**

Other titles by Sandra Marton available in eBook:

Harlequin Presents®

3026—THE ICE PRINCE *(The Orsini Brides)*
3032—THE REAL RIO D'AQUILLA *(The Orsini Brides)*
3056—SHEIKH WITHOUT A HEART

CHAPTER ONE

ALL HIS LIFE, Jake Wilde had been a man women wanted and men envied.

At sixteen, he was a football hero. He had his pilot's license. He dated the Homecoming Queen…and all the princesses in her court, one at a time, of course, because he had scruples—and because, even then, he understood women.

He was smart, too, and ruggedly good-looking, enough so that some guy had once stopped him on the street in Dallas to ask if he'd ever considered heading east to sign as a model.

Jake almost decked him until he realized it wasn't a come-on but a serious offer. He thanked him, said, "No," and could hardly wait to drive his truck back to his family's enormous ranch so he could laugh about it with his brothers.

In a word, life was good.

Time blurred.

College. Three years of it, anyway. Then, for reasons that made sense at the time, he'd enlisted.

One way or another, all the Wildes had served their country, Travis as a hotshot fighter pilot, Caleb as an operative in one of those alphabet-soup government agencies nobody talked about. For Jake, it had been the army and a coveted assignment, flying Blackhawk helicopters on dangerous missions.

Then, in a heartbeat, everything changed.

His world. His life. The very principles that had always defined him.

And yet—

And yet, some things did not change.

He hadn't quite realized that until a night in early spring as he tooled along a pitch-black Texas road, heading for home.

Jake scowled into the darkness.

Correction.

He was heading for the place where he'd grown up. He didn't think of it as home anymore, didn't think of any place as home.

He'd been away four long years. To be precise, four years, one month and fourteen days.

Still, the road seemed as familiar as the back of his hand.

So had the drive from the Dallas-Fort Worth airport.

Fifty miles of highway, the turn onto Country Road 227, the endless length of it bordered on either side by fence posts, the cattle standing still as sentinels in the quiet of night and then, almost an hour later, the bashed-in section of fence that seemed to have always marked the juncture where a nameless dirt road angled off to old man Chambers's spread.

And he'd only stopped to check for IEDs once.

A record.

Jake made the turn onto the road, even after all these years automatically steering the '63 Thunderbird around the pothole by the bashed-in fence that marked the Chambers boundary. It was on the old man's land, which was why nobody had filled it in.

"Don't need nobody messin' with my property," Elijah Chambers would mumble if anyone was foolish enough to suggest it.

Jake's father despised the old guy but then, the General despised anybody who wasn't into spit and polish.

Even his own sons.

You grew up with a four-star father, you were expected to lead a four-star life.

Caleb used to say that when they were kids. Or maybe it had been Travis.

Maybe it had even been him, Jake thought, and came as close to a smile as he had in a very long time, but he squelched it, fast.

A man learned to avoid smiling when the end result might scare the crap out of small children.

Jake drummed his fingers against the steering wheel.

Maybe his best move was to turn the car around and head for…

Where?

Not D.C. Not the hospital. If he never saw another hospital in his lifetime, it would be too soon. Not the base or his town house in Georgetown. Too many memories and besides, he didn't belong on the base or in D.C. anymore, and he'd sold the town house, signed the papers just yesterday.

The truth was, he didn't belong anywhere, not even here in Texas and absolutely not on the half million acres of rolling hills and grassland that was *El Sueño.*

Which was why he had no intention of staying very long.

His brothers knew it and were doing their best to talk him out of leaving.

"This is where you belong, man," Travis had said.

"This is your home," Caleb had added. "Just settle in, take it easy for a while, get your bearings while you figure out what you want to do next."

Jake shifted his weight, stretched his legs as much as he could. The Thunderbird was a little cramped for a man who stood six foot three in his bare feet, but you made sacrifices for a car you'd rebuilt the summer you were sixteen.

Caleb made it sound easy.

It wasn't.

He had no idea what he wanted to do next, not unless it involved turning back time and returning to the place where it had stopped, in a narrow pass surrounded by mountains that needled into a dirty gray sky….

"Stop it," he said, his voice sharp in the silence.

None of that.

He was going to spend a couple of days at

the ranch. See his sisters. His brothers. His father.

Then he'd take off.

Seeing his sisters would be great, as long as they didn't do anything stupid like tear up. The General? That would be okay, too. He'd probably give him a pep talk and as long as it didn't go on forever, he'd survive it.

As for his brothers…

To hell with it. There was nobody here to see what passed for a smile on his scarred face and the simple truth was, thinking about Caleb and Travis always made him smile.

The Wilde brothers had always been close. Played together as little kids, got into scrapes together as teens. For as long as any of them could remember, they'd always loved the same things. Fast cars. Beautiful women.

Trouble, with a capital *T*.

Peas in a pod, their sisters teased. Half sisters—the General had been married twice and the brothers and sisters had different mothers—and it was true.

Peas in a pod, for sure.

They were still close, even now, otherwise they wouldn't have been able to talk him into this visit—

Except, he'd done it on his own terms.

Well, more or less.

They'd wanted to send a jet for him.

"We have two of the damned things at *El Sueño*," Travis had said. "Hey, you know that better than we do. You're the guy who bought them, supervised their interior design, that whole bit. Why fly commercial if you don't have to?"

Why, indeed?

The part Travis hadn't mentioned was that Jake hadn't only bought the Wilde planes, he'd piloted them.

Not now.

A pilot with one functional eye wasn't a pilot anymore, and the thought of returning home as a passenger on a jet he'd once flown was more than he figured he could handle.

So he'd told his brothers he didn't know when he'd be able to leave, blah, blah, blah, and finally, they'd eased off.

"It'll be simpler all around if I just get in Friday evening and rent a car."

As if, he thought now, and smiled again.

He'd been paged as soon as he stepped into the Dallas-Fort Worth airport. He'd considered ignoring the page but finally he'd gritted his teeth and marched up to the arrivals desk.

"Captain Jacob Wilde," he'd said briskly. "You've been paging me."

The clerk behind the counter had her back to him. She'd turned, professional smile in place…

And blanched.

"Oh," she'd stammered, "oh…"

It had taken all his determination not to tell her that, yeah, despite the eye patch, she was looking at a face that was better suited to Halloween.

He had to give her credit. She'd recovered, fast. Got back her phony smile.

"Sir," she'd said, "we have something for you."

Something for him? What? It had better not be what some of the guys in the hospital had told him about, a welcoming committee of serious-faced civilians, all wanting to shake his hand.

No.

Thank God, it hadn't been that.

It had been a manila envelope.

Inside, he'd found a set of keys, directions to a particular parking garage…

And a note, his brothers' names scrawled at the bottom.

Did you really think you could fool us?

They'd left him his old Thunderbird to drive home.

It had been a crazy thing to do.

A damned crazy thing, indeed, Jake thought, and swallowed past a sudden tightness in his throat.

The car had made the miles through the endless expanse that was North Texas easier….

And, suddenly, there it was.

The wide gate that marked the northernmost boundary of *El Sueño.*

Jake slowed the car, then let it roll to a stop.

He'd forgotten what it was like, seeing that huge wooden gate, the weathered cedar sign that spelled out *El Sueño*—The Dream—in big bronze letters.

It was all the same, except for the fact that the gate stood open.

His sisters' idea, he was certain, a sweet way Lissa, Em and Jaimie had thought of to welcome him and remind him that this was his home. They'd be hurt when they realized home was the last place he wanted to be but he didn't see any way around it.

He had to keep moving.

He stepped hard on the gas and drove

through the open gate, a rooster tail of Texas dust pluming out behind him.

He wouldn't even have come this weekend, except he'd run out of excuses.

"Yeah. Well, I'll see what I can do," Jake had replied, and Caleb had said, very calmly, fine, good plan, and if he decided that what he *couldn't* do was come home for a visit then, by God, he and Travis would have no choice but to fly to D.C., hog-tie him and drag his sorry ass home.

For all he knew, they would have.

Jake had thought it over and decided it was time to show his face—and wasn't that one hell of an expression to use, he thought grimly.

It wouldn't come as a surprise to his family. They'd all been at the hospital, waiting, when the transport plane first brought him back to the States. His sisters, his brothers, even the General, reminding everybody he was John Hamilton Wilde, *General* John Hamilton Wilde, United States Army, and he damned well wanted a private room for his wounded son and the attention of the best surgeons at Walter Reed.

Jake had been too out of it to argue but as the days and weeks crawled by, as he came off the painkillers and his head began to function again, he'd laid down the law.

No more special treatment.

And no more family visits.

There was no point, no reason, no way he wanted to watch Em and Lissa and Jaimie trying to be brave, his brothers pretending he'd be back to himself in no time, his father being, well, his father.

That was one of the reasons he'd taken so long to come home, even for a visit.

"You're an idiot," Travis had growled.

Maybe.

But he didn't want to be fussed over, poked at, stroked and soothed and told nothing had changed, because everything had. His face. His sense of self.

Was he even a man anymore?

It was a damn good question.

A better one was, *How did you dance between the reality that everything was normal and the brutal knowledge that it wasn't?*

Forget that for now.

Tonight, his job was to put on a good show. Smile, as long as he didn't terrify anybody. Talk, even though he didn't have anything to say civilians would want to hear.

Behave as if time had not passed.

He'd figured coming to the ranch by himself would give him the chance to acclimate. Immerse himself in familiar things. Smell the clean Texas air and listen to the coyotes making their beautiful music in the night.

All of that without an unwanted rush of emotion engulfing him in a place like an airport.

Every solider he knew said the same thing.

Coming home was tough.

You went off to war, you were carried away by the excitement of it, especially if you'd been raised on stories of bravery and battles and warriors.

He sure as hell had.

Their mother was dead, gone when Travis was six, Caleb four, Jake two. Housekeepers, nannies and a stepmother, who'd only stayed long enough to bear three daughters, had raised them.

The General, the rare times he was home, regaled them with stories about their ancestors, a hodgepodge of men who'd marched on Gaul with Caesar, raided the British Isles from longboats, crossed the Atlantic in sailing ships and then conquered a vast new continent from the Dakota plains to the Mexican border.

The stories had thrilled him.

Now, he knew they were nonsense.

Not the part about the warriors. He'd been one himself these last years, fighting alongside honorable, brave men, serving a nation he loved.

But his father had left things unsaid. The politicians. The lies. The cover-ups.

Jake stood on the brakes. The Thunderbird skidded, slewed sideways across the dirt road and came to a hard stop. He crossed his hands on the steering wheel, wrist over wrist.

He could hear his heart thumping.

He was heading straight back into that dark place he'd sworn he wouldn't visit again.

He waited. Let his heartbeat slow. Then he opened the door and stepped from the car.

Something brushed against his face. A moth.

Good. Moths were real. They were things a man could understand.

He took a long gulp of cool night air. Tucked his hands into his trouser pockets. Looked up as clouds hid the stars, as cold and distant as the polar ice caps.

Minutes passed. The stars came out from behind the clouds, along with the moon. He got back into the 'Bird and drove on until, finally, he could see the outline of the house, standing on a rise maybe an eighth of a mile away.

Light streamed from its windows.

Panic twisted in his gut.

He pulled onto the grass, stopped the car again and got out.

There was a stand of old oaks to his left, and a footpath that led through them.

Jake set out along the path. A breeze carrying the gurgling sound of Coyote Creek winding, unseen, alongside, accompanied him. Dry leaves crunched under the soles of the cowboy boots he'd never given up wearing.

There'd been a time he'd loved nights like these. The crystalline air. The distant glitter of the stars.

Back then, he'd look up at the sky as he just had and wonder at the impossibility of standing on a planet spinning through space.

His hand went to his eye socket. The taut skin below it.

Now, the only thing a night like this meant was that the cold made his bones, his jaw, the empty space that had once been an eye, ache.

Why would the eye hurt when it didn't exist anymore?

He'd asked the doctors and physical therapists the question half a dozen times and always got the same answer.

His brain thought the eye was still there.

Yeah. Right.

Jake's mouth twisted.

Just went to prove what a useless thing a man's brain could be.

The bottom line was that it was cold and he hurt and why he'd got out of the 'Bird and set off on this all-but-forgotten ribbon of hard-packed dirt and moldy leaves was beyond him. But he had, and he'd be damned if he'd turn around now.

The trail was as familiar as the gate, the road, his old Thunderbird. It had been beaten into the soil by generations of foxes and coyotes and dogs, by ranch hands and kids going back and forth to the cold, swift-running waters of the creek.

Jake had walked it endless times, though never on a cold night with his head feeling as if somebody was inside, hammering to try and get out.

He should have taken something. Aspirin. A couple of pills, except he didn't want to take those effing pills, not even the aspirin, anymore.

By the time he emerged from the copse

of trees and brambles, he was ready to turn around, get in the car and head straight back to the airport.

Too late.

There it was.

The house, the heart of *El Sueño*, a brightly lit beacon. Sprawling. White-shingled. Tucked within the protective curve of a stand of tall black ash and even taller oaks, and overlooking a vast, velvety lawn.

Somewhere in the dark woods behind him, an owl gave a low, mournful cry. Jake shivered. Rubbed his eye. The skin felt hot to the touch.

The owl called out again. A faint, high scream accompanied the sound.

Dinner for the owl. Death for the creature caught in its sharp talons. That was the way of the world.

Some lived.

Some died.

And, goddammit, he was getting the hell out of here right now…

You can't run forever, Captain.

The voice was clear and sharp in his head.

Somebody had told him that. A surgeon? A shrink? Maybe he'd told it to himself.

It wasn't true. He could run and run and never stop—

The big front door of the house flew open.

Jake took a quick step back, into the shelter of the trees.

There were people in the doorway. Shapes. Shadows. He couldn't make out their faces. Music floated on the night air.

And voices.

Many voices.

He'd made it clear he wanted to see nobody but family.

A useless request.

His sisters would have invited half the town. The other half would have invited itself. This was Wilde's Crossing, after all.

Okay.

He could do this. He *would* do this.

Just for tonight because the truth was, deep in his heart, he still loved this place more than any other on earth. *El Sueño* was part of him. It was in his DNA as much as the Celtic ice-blue of his eyes, the Apache blackness of his hair. Centuries of Wilde blood pulsed through him with each beat of his heart.

"Dammit," he said in a soft growl.

He couldn't deny it—but he couldn't understand why it should matter. The past was the past. What did it have to do with the future?

Two different army shrinks had given him the same answer. The past was the basis of the present, and the present was the basis of the future.

Jake hadn't returned for any more lie-on-the-couch-and-vomit-out-your-secrets crap. He'd never given up his secrets to start with. What was the point of having a secret if you handed it off?

Besides, the shrinks were wrong.

The pain behind his eye, his nonexistent eye, had become a drumbeat. He rubbed the bone around it with a calloused hand.

He thought again of the stories he and his brothers had grown up on.

"Never forget," the General would say. "Everything we are, everything we have, we owe to the courage and convictions of all those brave men who came before us."

The brothers had all grown up waiting for the chance to carry on the tradition. College first, because their mother would have wanted it. Business management for Jake, law for Caleb, finance for Travis.

But Jake had been the only one who decided to become a soldier. He'd joined the army, longed for, and snagged, training flying Blackhawks, often on covert missions.

He'd loved it.

Taking out the enemy. Saving lives when nothing and nobody else could do it.

Suddenly, with gut-wrenching speed, he stood not in the dark Texas countryside, but in a place of blood and fire. Fire everywhere…

"No," he said sharply.

He drew a shaky breath. Straightened his long, tautly muscled frame and stood as tall as his aching head would permit.

He was not going to make that mental journey tonight.

Tonight, he would be the son his father had wanted, the man his brothers had known, the guy his sisters had adored.

The owl called out again. The bird was a hunter. A survivor.

Yeah, well, so was he.

He set off briskly over the night-damp grass, toward the house and the family that waited for him there. The moon was climbing higher. He felt its cool ivory light on his face.

The figures in the doorway grew clearer.

"Jake?"

Jaimie and Lissa cried out his name.

"Jake?"

Caleb and Travis shouted it.

"Jake," Emma shrieked, and just as he reached the house, they all came racing down the porch steps and engulfed him, laughing, crying. He felt dampness on his cheeks.

His brothers' tears. His sisters'.

Maybe even his.

CHAPTER TWO

A PROMISE MADE was a promise kept.

That was Addison McDowell's credo.

It was the only reason she was at this damned party tonight. She'd promised her financial advisor and her attorney—her Texas advisor and her Texas attorney—that she'd show up, so she had.

Doing what you said you would do was The Proper Thing. And doing The Proper Thing was important. She'd stuck with that ever since she'd decided that she was an Addison, not an Adoré.

Girls who grew up in run-down trailer parks might be given that awful name, but she'd left those days far, far behind.

She had become all that the name *Addison* implied.

She was successful. Sophisticated. She owned a Manhattan condo. Well, she had a fat mortgage on one, anyway. She had a law degree from Columbia University. She dressed well.

Only one fly in the ointment the last few months.

Her reputation was better suited to an Adoré than an Addison, and wasn't that one hell of a thing after all her efforts to escape that miserable trailer park and its sad heritage of silly, round-heeled women?

Addison raised her glass to her lips and took a sip of merlot.

If only Charlie had not left her that damned ranch.

If only he hadn't died.

He'd been the best friend she'd ever had. The only friend she'd ever had. He hadn't wanted her for her body, he'd wanted her for her intelligence, and to hell with what people thought.

Charles Hilton, the multimillion-dollar lawyer, had liked her. Respected her.

They'd begun as business associates, though she'd been only a junior member of his legal team, but as they'd gotten to know each other, Charlie had looked past the obvious: the glossy, dark hair she wore severely pulled away from her face; the silver eyes;

the curvy figure she did her best to disguise within severely tailored suits.

Charlie had seen the real her, the one with intelligence and the determination to succeed. He'd become her mentor.

She hadn't trusted his interest. Not at first. But as she'd gotten to know him, she'd realized that he loved her as the daughter he'd never had. In return, she'd loved him as the father she'd had and lost.

And when he'd grown frail and ill, she'd loved him even more because he'd needed her, and being needed was a wonderful feeling.

There had never been anything even remotely intimate between them, unless you counted rubbing his aching shoulders near the end of his life.

It was obscene even to consider.

But blogs and gossip columns didn't care about truth, not when fiction was so much more juicy, not in Manhattan or, as it had turned out, not in Wilde's Crossing, Texas.

She'd kept a low profile since coming to Wilde's Crossing, but that didn't mean a thing.

People watched her whenever she showed up in public.

She'd known tonight would be the same, no matter what the Wilde brothers said.

People would stare. Or try to be stealthy about it.

Either way, eyes would be on her.

"Wrong," Travis Wilde had said.

Addison sipped at her wine.

The one who'd been wrong was Travis.

She was getting lots of looks. And, hell, maybe she deserved them.

She'd started out wearing a business suit. Too New York, she'd decided; she'd stand out like the proverbial sore thumb.

So she'd ditched the suit for jeans, a silk blouse and boots.

A glance in old man Chambers's cracked bathroom mirror told her she looked like a New Yorker dressed for a Western costume party….

And wasn't it amazing that she'd fallen into calling Charlie's ranch, *her* ranch, by its former owner's name the way everybody else still did?

Finally, she'd looked in the mirror and said, "To hell with it."

The sound of her voice had set a mouse to scampering in the walls.

Good thing she wasn't afraid of mice, she'd

thought, or bugs, or the big snake she'd swept off the porch of the miserable pile of shingles she now owned.

She wasn't afraid of anything.

That was what had taken her from Trailer Park, USA, to Park Avenue, New York City.

So she'd changed to a black silk Diane von Furstenberg wraparound dress. It was very ladylike until you noticed how low the neckline dipped, and how the silk clung to her when she moved. Black kid, sky-high Manolo Blahniks were the finishing touch.

Another look in the mirror and she'd tossed her head.

Stories about her had reached Wilde's Crossing before she did.

When she'd questioned the Wildes, they'd both blushed.

The sight of grown men blushing had some charm, but Addison wasn't interested in charm. She was just damned tired of people talking about her.

Tonight, no matter what she wore, people would stare. Why not give them something to stare at, never mind that her dress and stilettos wouldn't have raised an eyebrow back home.

She'd suspected that most of the women

would wear jeans or what she thought of as tea dresses—frilly, flowery prints that only looked good on six-year-olds.

Right on all counts, Addison thought now, as she swapped her empty wineglass for a full one from the tray of a passing server.

Right about the women's clothes and the town's attitude. The women were the real pains in the ass because they weren't just judgmental, they were holier-than-thou.

Like the one watching at her right now.

Frilly dress? Check. Too much lipstick? Double check. And big hair. Did Texas wives not know that big hair looked good on Dolly Parton and nobody else?

Addison flashed the smile a cat might offer a mouse.

The woman flushed and looked away.

Pleased to meet you, too, Addison thought coldly, and then she also thought, *Why did I come here tonight?*

Because Travis and Caleb Wilde had asked her.

Back to square one.

They'd asked, and in a moment of uncharacteristic weakness, she'd told them she'd do it, she'd go to their brother's homecoming party, which wasn't supposed to be a party at all.

"Just family and a couple of old friends," Caleb had said.

"Well, maybe one or two more," Travis had added.

Right, Addison thought, with a mental roll of her eyes.

Just family and old friends. She should have known better. When Travis fell into that good-ole-boy drawl of his, anything was possible.

What looked like a zillion "old friends" had gathered in the enormous great room at *El Sueño.*

El Sueño. The Dream.

Addison hid a wry smile in her wineglass as she lifted it to her lips.

In Spanish or English, that was a pretty fanciful name for half a million acres of scrub, rolling grassland, flower and vegetable gardens, dusty roads, expensive horseflesh and gushing oil wells, but one of the things she'd discovered during the time she'd been here was that Texans could wax poetic about their land as easily as they could raise a sweat working it.

Even Charlie, who had not been a Texan

at all, but like her was a born and bred Easterner, though from a very, very different background, even he had somehow let the poetic part draw him in.

Not the sweat part.

It was impossible to imagine Charlie had ever raised a sweat on anything more labor-intensive than his stock portfolio.

Addison sighed.

Perhaps if he had, if he'd flown down to take a hard look at the Chambers ranch, ridden its seemingly endless dusty acres instead of relying on a picture-book spread in a fancy real-estate catalogue, he wouldn't have bought it.

But he had bought it, sight unseen, and died a week later.

Losing him had just about broken her heart—and then had come the shock of learning he'd willed her the ranch.

She'd done nothing about it for a while. Then, because the place had obviously been important to Charlie, she'd done what he hadn't.

She'd strung together all the vacation time she hadn't taken in two years, added this year's allotment and flown down to see it.

What she'd found wasn't a ranch at all, not

if you watched old John Wayne movies on late-night TV.

The Chambers place was umpteen thousand acres of scrub, outbuildings that looked as if a strong wind would topple them, a ranch house that had its own wildlife population, half a dozen sorry-looking horses and not very much else.

Which was the reason she had the Wildes as her advisors and—

"Now, little lady, how come you're drinkin' red wine when there's champagne flowin' like a stream to the Rio Grande?"

A big man wearing an even bigger Stetson, a flute of champagne in each oversize paw, flashed her a big smile.

Oh God, she thought wearily, *not again*.

"Jimbo Fawcett," he said. "Of the Fawcett Ranch."

How could somebody manage to tuck an entire pedigree into six words? Another Jimbo Fawcett look-alike already had, with the clear expectation that she'd want to spend the rest of the evening listening to him explain—with some modesty but not much because, after all, this was Texas—how incredibly lucky she was that he'd picked her out of the herd.

Except for the Stetsons, big-shot New York attorneys and Wall Street tycoons did it much the same way, so she was used to it.

"How nice for you," she said pleasantly.

"You jest got to be Addie McDowell."

"Addison McDowell. Yes."

Fawcett gave a booming laugh. "We're not so formal down here, little lady."

What the hell, Addison thought, enough was enough.

"Mr. Fawcett—"

"Jimbo."

"Mr. Fawcett." Addison gave him a bright smile. "In the next couple of minutes, you're going to tell me that I'm new to Wilde's Crossing and what a sad thing it is that we haven't met before."

Fawcett blinked.

"And I'm going to say yes, I'm new and we haven't met because I'm not interested in meeting anyone, and then I'll tell you that I prefer red wine and that I'm sure you're a nice guy but I'm not interested in champagne or anything else. Got it?"

Fawcett's mouth dropped open.

Addison took pity on the man and patted his arm.

"Thanks anyway," she said, and she turned

her back to him, wound her way through the crowd until she found an empty bit of wall space near a big Steinway grand piano and settled into it.

Dammit, she thought, glancing at her watch, how much longer until the local hero showed up? Five minutes more, and then—

"Why do I suspect you're not having a good time?"

Addison turned around, ready to provide a sharp answer, but when she saw the tall, good-looking man who'd slipped up next to her, she fixed him with a narrow-eyed glare instead.

"Travis Wilde," she said, "you owe me, big-time."

"Well, that answers your question," Caleb Wilde said as he joined them. "You suspect she's not having a good time because she isn't. Right, Addison?"

"Considering that I've spent the last months turning down invitations from the country club, the ranchers' association, the ladies' sewing league—"

"Not the sewing league," Travis said in shocked tones.

"The sewing league," Addison said, and when she saw the brothers' mouths twitch, she relented, if only a little. "You said he would be here by eight."

"Jacob." Caleb cleared his throat. "That's what we figured."

"It's almost eight-thirty. And there's still no sign of the mystery man."

"Jake's not a mystery man," Travis said quickly. "And he'll be here. Just be patient."

Addison made a face. The last few months, her patience had been in increasingly short supply.

"You need an expert to take a long, hard look at the Chambers place, figure out if it makes sense to fix it up before you put it on the market or not. In today's economic climate—"

Addison held up her hand.

"I've heard this speech before."

"It's still valid. Jake's recommendations could make hundreds of thousands of dollars' difference to you."

She could hardly scoff at that. Those Manhattan mortgage payments, the tuition loans…

Besides, the ranch had meant something to Charlie and he'd left it to her. That was a kind of obligation. She had to do the right thing with it, if only out of respect for his memory.

"Ten minutes. He'll be here by then," Caleb said. "Okay?"

"He'd better be," Addison said, but she softened the words with a smile.

She could spare another ten minutes, partly because she liked and respected Caleb, her attorney, and Travis, her financial consultant—

And partly because she was curious.

She was increasingly certain the Wildes weren't telling her all there was to tell about the mysterious Jacob.

She knew he was, or had been, in the army. That he'd been wounded. That he was some kind of hero. His brothers hadn't said so but she'd heard the rumors from the one lonely cowboy who worked her ranch part-time.

Caleb and Travis simply talked about his ability to assess the place.

"You sell it without his advice," they'd said, "you'll regret it."

"Couldn't someone else do it?" Addison had asked.

The brothers had exchanged a glance so quick she might not have noticed it if she hadn't been looking at them from across her desk—old man Chambers's desk—in what passed for the ranch office.

Addison's eyebrows had risen. "What?"

"Nothing," Caleb had said.

"Nothing at all," Travis had added.

"Bull," Addison had said calmly. "You're up to something and I want to know what it is."

Another of those quick looks. Then Travis had cleared his throat.

"Jake truly is the man you want, Addison."

Addison had been tempted to point out that she didn't want any man. She had a career she'd worked her tail off to obtain. But that wasn't what he'd meant, and she knew it.

"He's the best there is."

"But?"

Travis had shrugged. "But, he's not plannin' on stayin'."

"Here we go. The drawl. The smile. The famous Wilde charm—and you both know damned well how much good that will do you."

She'd said it just lightly enough so the brothers had chuckled.

"Heck," Travis had said, sitting back and crossing one boot-clad foot over the other, "it works with every other female in this part of Texas."

"I bet," Addison had said sweetly. "But I'm not from this part of Texas. I'm not from any part of Texas." She'd paused for emphasis. "And I'm not 'every other female,' I'm your employer."

"Our client," Travis had said, his drawl as lazy as Caleb's.

The brothers had grinned. So had Addison. It was a familiar routine and it still surprised her that she felt comfortable enough with them for relaxed banter.

"And because you're our client," Travis had said, "and we have your best interests at heart…."

"Try telling me all of it," Addison had said. "Or I'll put this place on the market tomorrow."

The brothers had exchanged a long look. Then Caleb sighed.

"Jake's been in the army."

"So?"

"So, he was, ah, he was wounded. And he, ah, he's not sure if he wants to stay at *El Sueño* or maybe move on. And—"

"And he needs a solid reason to stay," Travis had said bluntly, no charm, no drawl, nothing but the cool voice of the financial advisor Addison had come to know and respect. "He knows your land almost as well as he knows ours. He's smart, he's pragmatic, and he was born knowing horses and ranching."

"We promise you," Caleb had said in that same no-nonsense way, "you won't regret working with him." And then, before she could say anything, he'd added, "Have you had any regrets, dealing with us?"

Thinking back to that conversation, Addison sighed, brought her glass to her lips and drank some more wine.

No. She most definitely had no regrets. She'd learned not just to like the Wildes, but to trust them.

Travis had been her financial advisor pretty much since she'd arrived in Wilde's Crossing. Caleb had been her attorney close to the same length of time. Using a New York lawyer and a New York financial guru just hadn't made much sense.

The point was, she took legal advice from one Wilde and financial advice from the other.

It might make sense to take ranching advice from the other.

Which was why she was here, tonight.

Travis had greeted her; he'd taken her on the obligatory rounds, introduced her to his three sisters.

Apparently, no one had told them that her relationship with their brothers was strictly professional.

Not that they hadn't been pleasant, even gracious, but a woman could always tell when other women were sizing her up.

Listen, she'd almost said, *you can stop worrying. I do not, repeat, do not intend to sleep with either of your brothers. They're hunks, all right, and I like them, but I have no interest in getting involved with any man, no matter how handsome or sexy or rich or charming, not even if hell should freeze over.*

She wasn't interested in waiting another minute for the Hero to show up, either. The Wounded Hero, she reminded herself, but the wound could not have been much.

Jacob Wilde was a famous man's son. He would have grown up rich and spoiled—girls from trailer parks knew the type. So, why on earth was she still standing around, waiting for a man she would undoubtedly dislike on—

"Jake?"

"Oh, my God, Jake!"

Someone had opened the front door ten or fifteen minutes ago. Now the entire Wilde crew was trying to fit through it at once.

The sisters were shrieking and bouncing like yo-yo's. Caleb and Travis were laughing. The bunch of them exploded onto the porch, and the crowd moved in behind them for the show.

Addison sighed with resignation. Too late. She was stuck here, at least until she shook the hero's hand, or maybe he'd be so engulfed by the crowd that she'd be able to slip out without anybody noticing….

And then Jacob Wilde stepped into the room.

The breath caught in her throat.

She had expected him to be good-looking.

He wasn't.

He was—there was no other word for it—beautiful.

Tall. Broad-shouldered. A long, tautly muscled body, strong and straight in a uniform that bristled with ribbons. His hair was the color of midnight.

Corny, all of it, but true.

He had a face a sculptor might have chiseled.

A sculptor with a cruel sense of irony.

Because Jacob Wilde's face was perfect….

Except for the black patch over one eye, and the angry, ridged flesh that stretched across the arch of his cheek beneath it.

CHAPTER THREE

JAKE STOOD frozen in the open doorway.

The momentary rush of euphoria at seeing his sisters and brothers drained away as fast as the water from Coyote Creek in a dry Texas summer.

No party, he'd said. No crowd. And, yes, he'd figured there'd be people there anyway....

His belly knotted.

From where he stood, it looked as if the entire county had showed up.

He took a quick step back, or tried to, but his sisters threw themselves at him.

"You're here," Em said happily.

"Really here," Jaimie said.

"You're home," Lissa added, and what could he finally do but close his arms around them all?

Caleb pounded him on the back.

Travis squeezed his shoulder.

Despite everything, Jake began to grin.

"Is this a welcoming committee?" he said, "or a plot to do me in?"

They laughed with him, his sisters weeping, his brothers grinning from ear to ear.

For a few seconds, it was as if nothing had changed, as if they were all still kids and the world was a wonderland of endless possibilities....

Then Caleb cleared his throat.

"The General sends his best."

Jake checked the room. "He's not here?"

"No," Travis said uncomfortably. "He said to tell you he's sorry but he got hung up at a NATO meeting in London."

Reality returned in a cold, hard rush.

"Of course," Jake said politely. "I understand."

There was a moment of silence. Then Jaimie touched his arm.

"Everyone's waiting to say hello," she said softly.

Jake forced a smile. "So I see."

Caleb leaned in closer. "Sorry about the crowd," he murmured.

"Yeah," Travis said. "Trust me, bro. We didn't plan any of this."

"It's just that word got around," Lissa said. "And people were so eager to welcome you home…."

"You don't mind, Jake," Em said, "do you?"

"No," he said, "of course not."

His brothers saw right through the polite response. They exchanged a look.

"You ladies can have him later," Caleb said. "What he needs right now is a cold brew. Right, my man?"

What he needed was to get the hell out of here, especially because he knew what would happen once he stepped fully inside the room, where the lights were brighter and the crowd could get its first good look at him, but why add cowardice to his other sins?

"Unless," Travis said quickly, "baby brother wants champagne. Or wine."

Jake looked at his brothers. They were throwing him a lifeline, a way to grab hold of the past by segueing into an old routine.

"Champagne's for chicks," he said, the line coming to him as readily as his next breath. "Wine's for wusses."

"But beer—" Travis said solemnly.

Caleb finished the silly poem. "—is for real men."

Jake could almost feel his tension easing.

They'd come up with the doggerel years ago. It had been valid when they were in their teens. Not anymore. They'd all grown up; they'd traveled the world and, in the process, their tastes had become more sophisticated.

Travis even had a wine cellar, something they teased him about unmercifully.

Still, a cold beer sounded good, almost as good as the memories dredged up by the silly bit of shtick.

"A cold beer," Jake said wistfully. "A longneck?"

"Does real beer come in any other kind of bottle?"

The three Wildes smiled. And moved from the porch into the room.

"Hell," Jake muttered.

He'd forgotten the crowd. The lights.

The reaction.

People gasped. Slapped their hands to their mouths. Whispered to the person beside them.

Jake could have sworn that all the air in the big room had been siphoned away on one deep, communal inhalation.

"Crap," Caleb muttered. Travis echoed the sentiment, though with a far more basic Anglo-Saxonism.

"It's okay," Jake said, because if ever there'd been a time when a lie was a good thing, it was now.

A surge of partygoers surrounded him.

He recognized the faces. Ranchers. Their wives. The couple who owned the hardware store, the town's pharmacist. The owner of the local supermarket. The dentist. Teachers who'd known him in high school, coaches, guys he'd played football with.

Most of them had recovered their equilibrium. The men stuck out their hands. The women offered their cheeks for kisses.

All offered variations on the same theme.

Jake, it's wonderful to have you home.

"It's wonderful to be home," he answered.

Another lie, but what was he going to say? *No, it's not wonderful? I can't wait to get the hell out of here? I don't belong here anymore, I don't belong anywhere?*

"Just keep moving," Travis muttered.

Jake nodded. One foot in front of the other…

Who was that?

A woman. Standing all the way in the rear of the big room, near Em's piano.

He'd never seen her before.

If he had, he surely would have remembered her.

Tall. Slender. Dark hair pulled away from her face. An oval face that held a faint look of amusement.

In a sea of blue denim and pastel cotton, she wore black silk. Sexy black silk…

The crowd swelled, shifted, and he lost sight of her.

"You ready for this?"

"Ready for…?"

"The next bunch," Travis said, jerking his chin toward the larger crowd ahead.

"The cheers of your million fans," Caleb added, working hard for a light tone.

Jake forced a laugh, as he knew he was meant to do.

"Sure."

Two lies in two minutes. Had to be a record, even for him.

"Then, let's do it," Caleb said. "'Cause the sooner we make it to the end zone, the sooner we can get those beers."

A second laugh was more than he could manage. He smiled instead, took a deep breath and let his brothers lead him forward.

The crowd swallowed him up.

He shook more hands, returned more smiles,

did his best to ignore the glitter of tears in the eyes of some of the women, said, *Yeah, it was good to be back* and *Absolutely, it had been a long time* and finally, mercifully, he, Travis and Caleb reached the long trestle table that held platters of barbecued ribs and chicken wings alongside tiny sandwiches and bowls of tiny grilled vegetables.

"Real food and girl food," Caleb said, and this time, Jake's laughter was genuine.

"And the holy grail," Travis said, pulling three long-necked bottles from an ice-filled copper tub.

Jake took one, nodded his thanks and raised the bottle to his lips.

"Wait!" Caleb touched his bottle first to Travis's, then to Jake's. "Here's to having you home, brother," he said softly.

Was it time to point out that the toast was a little premature? No, Jake thought, and they clinked bottles, then drank.

The beer was cold and bitter, maybe what he needed to head off the still-throbbing ache behind his eye. Tension, the docs had said, and told him, earnestly, he had to learn to avoid stress.

Right, Jake thought, and took another long swallow.

"We've missed you."

He looked at Travis. "Yeah. Me, too."

"Hell," Caleb said, his voice gruff, "it just wasn't the same with you gone. This is where you belong, Jacob."

Okay. Jake could see where this was going.

"About that," he began, but Travis shook his head.

"We know. You're not staying. But you're here tonight. Let's just celebrate that, okay?"

The suggestion was harmless; it changed nothing. And the truth was, right now, it felt good to be with his family.

"Okay," he said, and then he smiled and touched his bottle to theirs again. "A toast to The Wilde Ones."

The old nickname made the brothers grin. And when Bill Sullivan from the feed store came up, clapped him on the shoulder and said, "Hey, Jake, great to see you," Jake shook hands, said whatever he was supposed to say….

Until, in a sudden break in the crowd, he saw the woman again.

He had a clearer look at her now, and more time to savor it.

Her hair was the color of rich coffee, thick and shiny; she'd pulled it back with something he couldn't quite make out, pins or maybe combs.

The style, if you could call it that, was simple...

So was the image that came into his head.

He could see her brushing those lush locks into submission. Her arms were raised, her breasts were thrust up so the nipples were elevated—

Elevated and ready for the whisper of a man's tongue, for the heat of his mouth...

"Jake?"

His groin tightened.

And that face.

Sculpted bones beneath creamy skin. Gray eyes. No. They were more silver than gray. A straight, no-nonsense nose above a mouth made for things best dreamed of in the deepest dark of the night....

"Jake?"

A hot rush of lust drove through his belly, so quick and fierce that it stunned him. He hadn't felt anything like it for a long time.

A very long time.

"Hey, man, where'd you go?"

He blinked himself back to reality, swung toward Travis, saw the plate of food he was holding out. Food was the last thing he wanted right now, but he took the plate and forced a smile to his lips.

"Just what I needed," he said briskly. "Thanks."

Travis and Caleb began eating. He did, too, though nothing he put in his mouth had any taste.

He wanted to turn around and look at the woman with the silver eyes.

Ridiculous, really.

What would be the point? Forget that moment of lust or hunger or whatever in hell it had been.

At most, it had been an aberration.

The unbelievable truth was that he wasn't into sex anymore, wasn't into wanting it or even thinking about it. His sex drive had gone south.

Like the eye, it simply wasn't there anymore.

Besides, he knew what he looked like. A guy with a Halloween mask for a face…

"…and damned if Lissa didn't say, 'Barbecue? *Barbecue?*' In that way she has, you know, of making you feel as if it's you who's crazy, not her?"

Travis laughed, so Jake laughed, too, but his thoughts returned to the woman.

And to the sudden certainty that she was watching him.

Slowly, with what he hoped was an elaborate show of disinterest, he glanced over his shoulder.

His pulse jumped.

She was. Watching him. Not with curiosity. Not with disgust.

With interest.

And she was alone.

Not in the sense that she was here by herself, though he was sure she was. What man would bring a woman who looked like this to a party and walk away from her?

What he meant was that she was alone in the full sense of the word, separate and apart from everyone and everything....

Except him.

He felt the sudden leap of his blood. And, once again, that urgent pull of desire.

Which was crazy.

Now? he thought. *In a room full of people?* His long-dormant libido was going to kick in and—holy hell—kick in and add a boner to the fright mask that already made him a standout in the crowd?

God knew, he'd tried to get a rise out of

himself—no pun intended—once his wounds had healed.

And fright mask or not, there'd been women who'd made it clear they'd have enjoyed his attention. Nurses. Therapists. A couple of pretty MDs. He had no idea whether it was out of pity or curiosity, or if, as one woman had whispered, that eye patch made him look hot....

The thing was, women had shown interest.

His reaction?

Nothing.

He might as well have been a monk. No erections, no steamy thoughts, not even an X-rated dream.

A few weeks ago, one of his doctors—the Shrink of the Month, was how Jake thought of it—had apparently figured out that he wasn't fully back in the land of the living.

"So, how's sex?" the shrink had suddenly asked.

Jake had given the kind of answer he'd hoped would end the discussion.

"Hey, Doc," he'd said with what he'd hoped was a careless grin, "you're over twenty-one. Find out for yourself."

His pathetic attempt at humor hadn't worked.

"Takes time for everything to function

again," the doc had said. "Not just physically. Emotionally. Trauma takes a toll, Captain, but you're young. You're healthy. Give yourself time and, you'll see, your sex drive will return."

"Sure," Jake had said.

But it hadn't.

Maybe he'd had too many other things to think about. What to do about his future. What to do about his past. How to get through the long days and longer nights.

Whatever the reason, sex—for a man who'd always had his pick of beautiful women—had suddenly become unimportant.

Desire, lust, call it what you liked, had not returned. He hadn't been with a woman since he'd been wounded, hadn't wanted to be with one....

Until now.

He took a deep breath. Told himself to look away from the brunette with the silver eyes, but he couldn't.

Not while she was looking at him.

He searched hard for that *oh-you-poor-thing* expression half the women in the room had showed him tonight.

It wasn't there.

She was simply watching him, assessing him with a steadiness that was unsettling.

His jaw tightened.

Now she was smiling, her lips curving in a way that reached deep into his gut.

She mouthed a word.

Hi.

And lifted her wineglass in…what could it be but invitation?

"Her name is Addison. Addison McDowell."

Caleb's voice was low. Jake looked at him.

"What?"

"The woman you're looking at."

"I wasn't looking at anybody."

Caleb raised an eyebrow. "Yeah, well, just in case you were—"

"I just told you, I wasn't."

"My mistake," Caleb said calmly. "I only meant—"

"What's she doing in Wilde's Crossing?"

His brothers exchanged a quick glance.

"She owns the Chambers ranch," Travis said.

Jake cocked his head. "What do you mean, she owns the Chambers ranch? The old man always said he'd never sell it. The General tried to buy it a dozen times, remember? And—"

"And got turned down. Well, the old guy died. Pretty much the way you'd expect, still working his skinny butt off, refusing help from anybody, his temper nasty as ever. Turned out he'd mortgaged the place to the hilt. The General found out, told his lawyer to buy it, but the bank had already turned it over."

"To her?"

"To some old rich guy from New York."

A muscle knotted in Jake's jaw.

"And she's the old rich guy's wife," he said flatly.

"The rich guy kicked the bucket right after he took ownership." Travis jerked his head toward the woman. "She inherited it."

"So, she's his widow."

"No."

"His daughter?"

"She was his friend."

Jake looked at the woman again. She was still watching him, her gaze unfaltering.

"Must have been his very good friend," he said coolly.

"Listen, man—"

"She doesn't look much like a rancher to me."

Travis laughed. "The understatement of the year."

"It doesn't help that the Chambers place is a disaster," Caleb said.

"It almost always was."

"Remember when we were kids and you worked there a couple of summers? You had lots of ideas about how to improve things."

"Yeah, well, old man Chambers didn't want to hear any ideas but his own."

"Addison would."

Jake looked at Caleb. "Addison?"

"She's a friend."

Jake brought his beer to his lips and took a long swallow. Why was the taste of it more bitter than before?

"Woman looks like that probably has a lot of 'friends.'"

"She is," Caleb repeated, his tone as cool as Jake's, "exactly what I said. A friend."

"Whatever you say."

"Dammit, Jacob—"

"The point is," Travis said quickly, "we thought you might help her."

Jake almost laughed. He wasn't having

much luck helping himself, much less somebody else.

"You know, take a look at the land, the buildings—"

"Here's the deal, Trav. I'm leaving tomorrow."

"We figured it would be something like that. Well, no sweat. Check the property for her, leave next week instead. A business deal."

"Is that what you call your arrangement with her? A business deal?"

Why in hell had he said that? What did his brother's relationship with a woman he'd never met—and never would meet—matter?

He saw Travis's eyes narrow and he put out his hand and squeezed his shoulder.

"Sorry." He managed a quick smile. "I guess I'm not used to talking to people who aren't wearing cotton nightgowns that leave their butts hanging out."

"As a matter of fact, the answer is yes. She's my client. Caleb's, too. I'm her financial consultant. He's her lawyer. She's a smart, tough broad. An attorney, like Caleb, but from New York. If I were you, I wouldn't underestimate her."

No. A man would be foolish to underestimate a woman who could pin him with a look.

"No danger of that," Jake said. "I told you, I'm not staying, so you'd best not recommend me to—"

"We already did. Well, hell, why wouldn't we? We told her you were the man she wanted. She's, ah, she's damn near convinced."

Jake wasn't listening. He was watching the woman again. And as he did, she raised her glass of wine to her lips, sipped at the ruby liquid, then ran the tip of her tongue over her lips.

A soft, low sound formed in the back of his throat.

"Jake? You okay?"

"I'm fine," he said, his gaze never leaving her.

"Did you hear what I said? She's pretty much convinced."

"Convinced of what?"

"That you're the guy for her."

"That I'm—"

Caleb rolled his eyes. "That you're the man she should hire. See how she's looking at you? She probably figures we're telling you about her." He gave a quick, all-too-cheerful laugh. "We told her she'd have to turn on the charm, come up with somethin' special to convince you to—"

Travis, watching Jake's face, said, "Caleb," in a sharp, low voice.

"Something special," Jake repeated carefully.

"And she will. She's one hell of a resourceful female, Jake. If she decides she wants to grab your attention—"

"Dammit, Caleb," Travis growled. "Will you shut up?"

"Wait a minute, okay? I'm explaining things here. Jake needs to know this is all about business, that Addison's all about business..." His voice trailed off. "Jake?"

"Jake!" Travis called, but Jake was already shouldering his way through the crowd, anger churning in his belly where, moments before, there'd been heat.

CHAPTER FOUR

AT NINE, Addison had run away from home.

She'd done it before.

No special reason, just the childish hope that somewhere out there was a place where people read books instead of watching soap operas, where your mother didn't spend hours putting curls in her hair and paint on her nails and then, though you hated it, doing those same things to you.

That time, instead of heading for the highway, she'd cut through the woods that led into the mountains.

Branches had slapped at her face, brambles had torn her shirt and jeans.

At last, she'd emerged into a clearing. And found herself face-to-face with a mountain lion.

The big cat had put back its ears and snarled.

Addison's heart leaped. She knew a lot

about mountain lions. They were fast. They were unpredictable. They were beautiful and intelligent….

They were also incredibly dangerous.

Adrenaline pumped through her muscles. *Run*, every instinct said.

Fortunately, her head knew better. Showing weakness would be the kiss of death.

So, though she was terrified, she'd held her ground. And—such a silly cliché—time stood still.

How else to describe what happened when predator and prey confronted each other?

Now, almost two decades later, she flashed back to that memory. She hadn't run and after what had seemed like hours, but had surely been only seconds, the cat had turned and bounded away.

Jacob Wilde was coming toward her, and he looked every bit as dangerous as the mountain lion.

Until a few minutes ago, he'd watched her with an intensity that had been… What was the word? Disconcerting. His brothers had been talking to him. About her, she'd assumed, from the way he, then they, had looked at her.

She'd waited for something to happen.

For Travis and Caleb to bring him over to introduce him. Or for him to acknowledge her with a smile, a nod.

She'd waited. And waited. His stillness baffled her. Annoyed her.

Irritated her.

Was he expecting her to make the first move?

Okay, she'd finally decided, *why not?* She'd smiled. Raised her glass. She'd done all she could to convey the message, *Hello, I'm Addison and you're Jake, and though I don't think we'll really do business together, we probably should at least meet to make your brothers happy....*

And then everything changed.

His jaw tightened. His mouth thinned. A hot, hungry look swept across his face.

She knew that look. It was one of pure sexuality.

She hated when men looked at her like that. They always had, from the time she'd first grown breasts.

See that, baby girl? her mother would say. *Boys like you. Isn't that nice?*

It wasn't, not when you knew, even then, that you wanted to make it on your intelligence, not on whatever it was boys liked.

So, yes, she hated that look men got....

Except, this time, a stranger looked at her the way a starving man would look at a steak, and she felt her knees go weak.

It shocked her. Flustered her. She felt breathless.

She'd tried to deal with it by changing focus.

She'd taken a mouthful of wine....

And everything had gone to hell.

His brothers said something. Jacob Wilde swung toward them. There was a fast, obviously unpleasant exchange of words.

And then he'd headed straight at her, and all she could think of was that mountain lion and how she'd felt when it had turned its savage eyes on her....

Except, he wasn't a lion and she wasn't a scared kid, and she'd be damned if she'd let him intimidate her.

The thing was, it was all happening in slow motion.

His single-minded approach.

His brothers hurrying after him.

"Jake," Caleb called. "Jake, wait a minute!"

"Dammit," Travis said, "you're making a big mistake."

By now, heads were turning. People were staring. That was the last thing she needed.

A public scene over who-knew-what when she'd spent the past weeks doing everything she could to avoid public *anythings*!

Okay.

She took a step back.

Forget facing the lion. Forget refusing to be intimidated. The man was crazy, and she was absolutely not going to permit him to—

Too late.

His hand, hard as steel, wrapped around her wrist.

"Going somewhere?" he said in a low voice.

Addison's heart was racing. It was difficult to speak calmly, but she did.

"Let go of me."

"Why? My brothers said you were eager to meet me."

"Hardly eager." Her gaze went from his face to her wrist, then back again. "Are you deaf? I said—"

"Deaf as well as blind?" He smiled thinly.

"No, Miss McDowell. One disability at a time is my limit."

She winced. The guy was a nut-job but she had no intention of insulting him.

"I can assure you, I didn't mean—"

"No. And you can also assure me you didn't tell my brothers how much you wanted to meet me."

"Jake," Travis said in a warning tone.

Addison looked past Jacob Wilde. His brothers had positioned themselves slightly behind him, one on either side. They seemed ready to grab him and march him away.

The idea should have been comforting. It wasn't. All three Wildes were big and strong and hard-bodied, but she had no doubt that this one's icy rage would surely give him an edge.

Maybe a calm approach would work.

"I told them I'd agree to meet you," Addison said. "It seemed to mean a lot to them."

"You *wanted* to meet me," he said coldly. "And when they told you they knew damned well I wasn't going to be interested in taking you on as a client—"

"A client?" Her eyes narrowed. "What they wanted was for me to give you a job."

"The hell they did."

Addison felt her resolve to stay calm slipping.

"They close to begged me to give you a reason to hang around."

"Right," Jake snapped. "That's why you went into that—that routine."

What was he talking about?

"Look," she said carefully, "I think there's been a misunderstanding—"

"The look. The smile. That last little touch, the sip of wine and that sexy lick of your lips."

"You," she said flatly, "are a lunatic."

"Holy hell," Caleb growled, "Jake. Man, you've got this all wrong."

Jake ignored him.

"Has it ever failed you before, or is this a first?"

Addison stared at him. The ridged scars below the black eye patch were red and angry-looking.

She felt a twinge of compassion.

His visible wounds were brutal. Maybe they went even deeper. Was his behavior yet another indication of what he'd gone through?

He'd sacrificed for his country. For people like her. If he'd come away from the war with some idiosyncrasy, some behavioral tic—

"Don't," he said sharply.

"I beg your pardon?"

"Don't look at me as if I were a dog lying by the side of the road." His hand tightened on her wrist; he gave a little twist that brought her to her toes and she gave a soft, inadvertent gasp. "I don't need your pity any more than I needed your come-on."

So much for compassion.

"Come-on? You think I—" Addison glared at his brothers over Jake Wilde's shoulder. "Get your lunatic brother away from me," she said through her teeth, "and do it fast!"

"Jacob," Travis said, "let's go outside, okay? Get some fresh air—"

"Jake," Caleb said, "man, let go of the lady."

The certifiably insane Wilde brother didn't respond. Then, after what seemed an eternity, he dropped his hand from hers.

She wanted to look and see if his fingers had left marks, but she'd sooner have let her hand fall off than give him the satisfaction.

"I want to be sure you get the message, Ms. McDowell," he said. "You can pull out all the stops. I still won't assess the Chambers ranch."

"It's not the Chambers ranch. It's mine. And I'd sooner see the place dry up and blow away before I'd let you step on it."

He flashed a cold smile.

"It's yours because you managed to con a sick old man into buying it for you."

"You," Addison said, "are a horrible man."

"Why? Because I'm not an easy mark the way he was?"

Travis and Caleb groaned. Addison's gaze flew to them again and seared them with fire.

"My, oh, my," she said with a deadly calm, "you boys had quite an interesting chat."

"Addison," Travis said, "if you're suggesting—"

"What I'm 'suggesting,'" she snapped, "is that I'd sooner take advice from Elsie the cow than from this—this all-ego, no-brains brother of yours."

"Listen, lady—"

"No," Addison said, "*you* listen!" She took a quick step forward, lifted her chin, slapped her hands on her hips and glared. "Your brothers spent hours trying to sell you to me. You were a genius. You were brilliant. You—

you were in communion with the soil and the grass and the horses—"

"Jake," Caleb said quickly, "man, we never—"

"One look at my ranch, they said, and, poof, you'd know exactly what it needed."

"And?"

"And even though I didn't see any point to getting your assessment of something any fool can see is a disaster, I thought—*thought*," she said coldly, glaring at Travis and Caleb again, "that I could trust them."

"You can," Travis said quickly. "We never—"

"And," Addison said, ignoring the interruption, "because I was also foolish enough to believe your brothers were my friends, I said, okay, I'd give the Ranch Guru five minutes of my time."

Jake wanted to laugh. Ridiculous, when he was so ticked off. Instead, he folded his arms over his chest.

"How generous," he growled.

"Addison. Jake. You guys are both—"

"Which is why," Addison continued, with a withering glace at Caleb, "*which* is the *only* reason I came to this—this hail-the-conquering-hero party where I endured being hit on by every dumbass cowboy over the age of twelve, and the way the women looked at me, as if my sole purpose in life was to steal their homely, fat, drooling husbands."

Travis made a choking sound. Caleb rubbed his forehead. Jake had a hard time keeping from doing the same.

"And I waited, patiently, for the main event."

"The what?" Jake said.

"The main event, Captain. You. I waited and waited, and you finally showed up, but did your sainted sisters or your magnificent brothers introduce us?"

"Our sisters don't know anything about this," Travis said. He looked around. "And could we take this in another room? We really don't need an aud—"

"I watched the three of you standing there, swilling beer—a disgusting beverage but then, what could anyone expect from Texans?"

Dammit, Jake thought, the McDowell woman was some piece of work. Beautiful. Tough. And flawlessly delivering insult after insult, as if this whole thing wasn't her fault.

It was, of course, and he disliked her intensely, but he had to admire her for her guts.

"Beer, from the *bottle*," she added, with a visible shudder. "And you looked at me. Talked about me." Addison extended her hand, poked Jake in the chest. He jumped in surprise. "Although actually, Captain, you didn't look. You stared."

He felt heat rise in his face. "I did not stare."

"Oh, please! You stared. And when I got tired of it, tired of cooling my heels and waiting for you to come over, you know, do the polite thing, introduce yourself, shake my hand, I thought, okay, if he doesn't have any manners, I do. So I gave you a little salute."

Jake frowned. The raised wineglass?

"I even smiled."

Yes. Yes, she'd smiled, but—then she'd taken that slow, sexy sip of vino…

"You didn't so much as blink, so I drank a little wine to give you the chance to start moving in my direction."

Caleb cleared his throat.

"Addison, if you'd calm down—"

"I am calm," she said coldly. "Very calm. And, by the way, the two of you are fired."

"Why fire them? I'm the one you're ticked off at."

"Your DNA is their DNA. That's good enough for me."

"That's brilliant."

"It is, indeed."

"Well, that's fine. Because if you've dumped my brothers, there's no need for me to hold back."

Addison barked out a laugh.

Jake's mouth thinned.

"That ranch you own? It's worth exactly what you paid for it." He smirked. "Unless, of course, you put a higher price on what you gave the poor sucker who left it to you than those services were truly worth—"

Addison slapped his face.

Hard.

The imprint of her hand stood out on his cheek in crimson relief.

"Oh, man," Travis said, but the words were lost in the sound of a hundred shocked party guests dragging air into their lungs all at the same time.

"No wonder your brothers want to keep you where they can see you," she said. "You can't be trusted in polite society."

His dumbfounded expression told her she'd just scored a perfect shot.

Why hang around and ruin it?

Addison turned her back and faced the crowd.

"Move," she said, and a path opened like the parting of the Red Sea.

She stomped down that path…and stopped, halfway to the front door. *What the hell*, she thought, and she turned to face him one last time.

"You're also a nasty, egotistical, despicable jerk."

The crowd gasped again, then erupted in a frantic buzz of delighted whispers.

She'd given Wilde's Crossing enough to talk about for the next decade.

So what?

She was out of here. Not just the Wilde house. She was out of the town, out of the state of Texas.

Back home, at least, she knew the enemy. She wouldn't be taken in by a pair of brothers who looked like they'd stepped out of an old John Wayne movie, or by a man so tragically beautiful he'd made her heart ache.

Someone stepped out in front of her. A Wilde sister, Emma or Lissa or whatever in hell her name was.

"Miss McDowell. Please—"

"It's Ms. McDowell. And you have my deepest sympathy."

Addison stepped around the sister, yanked open the door and stepped into the night.

* * *

Travis and Caleb watched her go.

Then they looked at each other, grabbed Jake by the elbows and quick-marched him in the other direction, out the French doors that led to the patio.

"You," Caleb said, "are an effing idiot."

"You two are the idiots," Jake snarled. "Thinking a woman like that could use her wiles to keep me in town—"

"Her wiles," Travis said to Caleb. "He thinks we set it up so Addison would use her wiles." His dark blue eyes narrowed. "Nobody's used their 'wiles' since the nineteenth century, Jacob. And even if she had wiles, do you really think we'd ask her to use them?"

"Listen, I understand. You want me to hang around. And she's a hot piece of—"

"She's our friend," Caleb said coldly. "At least, she was, until you got your nose out of joint because you realized she wasn't coming on to you."

Jake reddened.

"Why would I want her to come on to me?"

His brothers barked out matching laughs.

"Okay, she's good-looking. But she was only coming on to me to get me to work for her."

"Not even you can possibly believe that."

Jake thought about it. And felt his belly start to knot.

"Okay. Maybe I, ah, maybe I overstated it, but—"

"Here's how it went down, Jake. You *wanted* her to come on to you. And when you found out she wasn't, you were too damned ticked off to admit that was what you wanted, so you decided to *accuse* her of coming on to you."

"That," Jake said coldly, "makes no sense at all."

"It makes more sense than you do," Travis said grimly.

"Hey. Just because your plan didn't work—"

"Goddammit," Caleb said, "she was right. You're an egotistical jerk."

Jake opened his mouth.

And shut it again.

His brothers had tempers. Hell, so did he. They'd chewed each other out before….

But never like this. Never with such intensity…

And maybe never with such honesty.

Were they… Could they be right?

"We owe her an apology," Travis told Caleb, who nodded.

"That's if she'll accept one."

"Let's go," Travis said…and Jake held up his hand.

"Wait, okay?" He cleared his throat. "So, ah, so this wasn't a setup."

"Lucky for you that you didn't make that a question," Caleb said grimly.

"Okay. Maybe I went…overboard. Maybe I read things into things—"

Travis snorted.

Jake ran his hands through his hair. "Ah, man, she's right. I am certifiable. It's just… it's been a while since—a while since…" He shook his head. "You guys don't owe her an apology. I do."

"She won't talk to you."

"She will."

"She won't. She's tough."

Jake eyed his brothers. "Trust me," he said. "I'm not exactly made of spun sugar."

"You mean," Caleb said innocently, "you're not a candy ass?"

Jake grinned. "Ten bucks says she'll not only accept my apology, she'll agree to have dinner with me tomorrow night."

"Twenty," Travis said, "and you're on."

The brothers smiled at each other. Jake started off the patio, toward the side of the house, then turned back.

"I left my car near the creek."

"Why'd you—"

"He just did," Caleb said.

"Oh. Fine." Travis dug the keys to his truck from his pocket and tossed them to Jake. "It's the black Tundra in the driveway."

"Remember," Jake said. "Twenty bucks."

His brothers grinned. "All talk, no action."

It was one of their old lines. Jake laughed on cue….

But his laughter died by the time he reached Travis's Tundra.

For a little while there, he'd almost forgotten.

All talk, no action was no longer a punch line. It was the sad truth. His brothers couldn't know it but he did.

And, yeah, that was the reason he'd gone ballistic. He'd responded to a woman for the first time in almost two years….

Only to find out that she wasn't interested.

Definitely, he owed her an apology. As for asking her to dinner…

Jake put the truck in gear and his foot on the gas.

Forget it.

He'd pay his brothers the twenty bucks and write the whole thing off as a mistake.

CHAPTER FIVE

CLOUDS HAD swallowed the moon and stars, turning the road into an inky ribbon that stretched toward infinity.

Addison had a head start but Jake drove fast, all but flooring the gas pedal. Every now and then, her taillights glowed crimson-bright ahead of him, but whenever the road curved, those lights disappeared.

She was driving fast, too. Dangerously so. Was she accustomed to dirt roads? Her world was surely one of limousines and taxis.

It surprised him that she could handle a car with such authority but then, everything about her surprised him.

He'd never seen such anger in a woman. Such fire.

And his stupidity had fueled it.

Jake frowned.

Talk about a man making fool of himself…

"Hell," he muttered.

Apologizing wasn't going to be easy. How did a man look a woman in the eye and say, "Okay, I'm an ass." Or, better still, exactly what she'd called him, an arrogant jerk.

What kind of justification could he come up with to explain his behavior?

Not the truth.

Not that that second he'd seen her, he'd wanted her, that he'd reacted to her in a way he'd all but given up thinking he'd ever react to a woman again—

That believing she'd put on an act had all but destroyed him.

There wasn't a way in the world he could admit any of that to her.

Nothing showed ahead of him but the bright tunnel created by the Tundra's headlights. He goosed the gas, the truck shot forward and his reward was another quick wink of red taillights.

"Wilde," he said through his teeth, "she's right. You're an idiot."

Maybe he'd be lucky.

Maybe a simple "I'm sorry, I was wrong," would be enough.

Right.

And she'd tell him, in explicit terms, precisely what he could do with those words.

Jake flexed his hands on the steering wheel.

This was not going to be fun.

He could imagine how she'd look while he stumbled through an apology.

Her cheeks would be pink with anger, her eyes as bright as molten silver. That I-can-take-on-the-world chin would be lifted to an angle that spelled defiance.

She'd be a veritable portrait of rage.

And sexy as hell.

Just thinking about it made his temperature rise and, hell, that was *not* what he wanted right now.

He had to concentrate on how to approach her. What to say. He worked on that while the truck ate up the miles, but nothing logical came to him.

He'd have to play it by ear.

And she'd make him jump through hoops.

That was the one certainty.

A muscle knotted in his jaw.

There was a time he'd have looked forward to the challenge. A woman, standing up to him? Except for a couple of tough-as-nails nurses who'd taken him on when he'd tried to refuse meds or therapy, women had always tended to say yes to whatever he wanted.

No surprise there.

If a guy had money, some kind of status, if he had the kind of looks women liked, that was the way things went.

He—for that matter, he *and* his brothers—had all those things.

For starters, they'd been born to money. Their father's, sure, but beyond that, their mother had left each of them a hefty trust fund.

Jake had let his sit in the bank. Then he'd wised up and invested it with Travis.

Even now, driving through the night in pursuit of a woman who'd probably love nothing more than to kick him where he lived, remembering how he'd done it made him smile.

He'd cornered his brother the night before he shipped out the first time and handed him a check.

Travis, who'd been just starting up his own financial firm, had looked at the sum, then at Jake. He gave a soft whistle.

"You want me to handle it all?"

"Every dollar."

"Risk…or no risk?"

Jake's reply had been a grin. Travis had grinned, too, and the deal was made.

Jake had pretty much forgotten about it after that. When you were busy keeping your ass from getting shot off, money wasn't much on your mind.

He came home on leave, Travis handed him a statement. That time, Jake was the one who'd whistled.

His seven figures had tripled. God only knew what it had grown to by now, despite the tough economic times.

As for status…

He was the son of a general. That was big, but in Texas, being the son of the man who owned *El Sueño* was even bigger.

Still, Jake had acquired his own kind of status early on.

At sixteen, he'd been a star high school quarterback. At eighteen, half a dozen top schools had offered him scholarships. At nineteen, pro scouts were already looking at him.

And at twenty, he'd walked away from college and football to enlist in the army, where he'd flown into the heart of battle.

As for his looks…

It was that DNA thing again.

He was tall. Lean. Muscular. His nose had a bump in it, courtesy of a burly defensive lineman, but that didn't work against him at all.

Women went for the entire package.

His hands tightened on the steering wheel.

He still had the money. The status. The looks…?

He didn't much care.

He knew his wounds made people uncomfortable. Like tonight. People looked at him, they flinched, they averted their eyes, they showed pity.

Pity was the worst of all.

As for seeing his own face in the mirror every morning—it was still a shock, but not because of vanity. It was a shock because it was a constant reminder of his failure.

"You need to give that up, Captain," one of the shrinks had told him. "Get a prosthetic eye. Let people—let *yourself*—see the real you."

What reality had to do with popping an artificial eyeball into what was, basically, a hole in his head didn't make sense even if the shrinks thought it did.

"Have you ever considered that it counteracts the medal you were awarded?" one had said, and Jake had ignored that for the stupid comment it was.

And all of this was pointless to think about, especially—

"Holy hell," Jake said, and stood on the brakes.

A deer and her yearling stood twenty feet ahead of him, big eyes filled with innocence as they stared at his truck.

He dragged in a breath.

"Go on," he said. "Get out of the way."

The animals remained motionless. Then mama flicked her tail and she and the baby ran into the scrub.

Jake started the truck again.

He'd been lucky not to have hit the deer. His fault, entirely. Antelope, deer, coyotes all used the road, especially at night.

His head had been everywhere except where it should have been….

And the glow of Addison McDowell's tail-lights was history.

No problem.

She was heading for the Chambers ranch and so was he.

A few minutes later, he bounced over the familiar pothole that signaled the start of Chambers land.

He slowed, took a good look at the gate and saw what he hadn't seen the first time. It wasn't locked. Truth was, the thing was barely a gate. Crossbars, posts, a couple of broken hinges. The gate hung open, swaying drunkenly in the breeze, looking more like kindling than anything else.

Jake eased the truck forward, nosed it through the opening, then started up the long gravel drive to the house.

Still no taillights.

If the McDowell woman had already reached the house, what did he do?

Park? Go to the door and knock? Or did he sit in the truck and tap on his horn? He had the feeling turning up, unannounced on her doorstep, might not be the best—

Light blazed through the windshield, blinding him. Jake cursed, flung his arm in front of his face, and for the second time in minutes, stood on the brakes.

The truck came to a hard stop.

What was he looking at? Headlights? The light from a big flashlight? No way could he see past it.

Cautiously, he opened his door.

"Ms. McDowell?"

Nothing. Just the darkness, the silence and the light.

"Addison? Are those your headlights? Turn them off."

Still nothing. Jake squinted hard. He took a step to the left. The brightest light remained focused on the Tundra but another light followed him.

Headlights and a flashlight. Addison—it had to be her—was using both.

He couldn't see a thing.

"Hey," he shouted. "Didn't you hear me? Turn off those lights."

Still no response. Jake grunted, moved another few steps from the truck….

The flashlight beam settled on him and held.

The hair on the back of his neck stood up. He'd had enough of being a living target to last him a lifetime.

"Turn that thing away from me," he said coldly. "Do it now."

Survival instinct, honed in a place thousands of miles and many centuries away, kicked in.

This wasn't Texas anymore.

Jake dropped to the ground and rolled, not

toward the truck as the enemy might predict, but away from it, into scrub and darkness.

Everything in him focused on that beam of light.

His heart rate slowed. The sounds of the night faded; he could hear his opponent's breaths.

The beam of light moved. Swept over the truck. Over the ground. It was searching for him.

Jake rolled again. Pressed himself to the earth ten or twelve feet from the road.

Wait, he told himself. Wait for the right instant, for the opportunity that always presented itself if you were ready....

"Show yourself," a voice called.

Addison McDowell's voice.

It shot him back to reality. This wasn't some hell-begotten dirt track in Afghanistan, it was Texas. And the person with the flashlight wasn't the enemy, it was simply a woman who'd been frightened by the headlights following her home.

He let out a long breath.

"Addison. Hey. It's Jake Wilde. You don't have to—"

The beam of light swept over the road, the

truck, the scrub. It would find him soon. Jake started to rise.

"Addison? Listen, I understand why you're upset—"

"All you need to understand is that I have a gun. And I damn well know how to use it."

Jake dropped to his belly, fast. A gun? Impossible. Where would she get a…

From the Chambers house, of course. The old man had kept a dozen guns, rifles, shotguns, automatics. He'd been the worst kind of hunter, shooting anything that moved.

Hell.

This wasn't good.

Jake cleared his throat.

"Addison. I'm not here to hurt you."

"I'm going to start counting, Captain. By the time I get to five, you'd better be on your feet with your hands in the air."

"Did you hear me? You don't want to have an accident with that thing—"

"Shooting you won't be an accident."

"Goddammit, woman—"

The light swept past him.

"One," she said. "Two."

It came to a stop, inches from his head.

"Wait. Listen to me. All I want is—"

"I know exactly what you want."

He blinked.

There was no mistaking what she meant. The only response he could think of was "uh-oh," but he had the feeling that wasn't going to do it.

"You're wrong," he said quickly. "I don't—"

"Three," she said, no hesitancy in her voice at all.

Jake took a breath, shot to his feet, focused his sight to the left of the light in hopes it wouldn't blind him and ran to where he figured she was standing.

He hit her, hard, just as he'd planned, his shoulder driving into her with enough force to take them both to the ground.

The flashlight flew from her hand.

Then she was under him, legs spread, arms raised, fingers clawing for his face. He grunted, grabbed for her wrists and struggled to immobilize her.

Her knee came up. She didn't have a lot of leverage but she jammed it into his groin anyway, hard enough to make him gasp.

He flung himself against her, pinned her with his body, his hands clasping hers, holding them out to the sides.

"Listen to me," he said roughly. "I'm not here to hurt—"

She struck like a snake, head coming up, teeth sharp as tiny knives sinking into his throat.

He jerked back.

"For God's sake, woman, will you listen?"

"I'll kill you," she gasped. "So help me, I'll—"

"I came to apologize."

"You do this to me, I swear—"

"I came here to apologize, dammit!"

She grunted. Wriggled. It was like wrestling with a wildcat....

Except, this was a woman.

Warm.

Lithe.

Silken.

They were two people in deadly combat—and yet, despite that, despite everything, Jake felt his duplicitous body coming alive.

Her hair smelled of flowers. Lily of the valley. Lilacs. He didn't know enough about flowers to be able to identify the scent, he only knew that its fragrance was delicate and surprisingly old-fashioned.

Her breath was warm. Wine-scented. Her mouth would taste rich and sweet.

Her breasts were soft. God, *she* was soft. Sweet and soft. He thought what it would be like to sink into her, sink deep, have her wrap her legs around him.

In a heartbeat, he was aroused and erect and hard as a rock against her.

"Crap," he growled, and he rolled away, shot to his feet, turned his back, stood with his head bent, his hands on his hips, his breathing rough and rapid.

The names she'd called him didn't half cover the territory.

If Addison McDowell really did have a gun, she might as well shoot him because he was worthless. A man who'd get turned while a woman fought him in terror…

He took a long breath, expelled it and swung toward her.

She'd risen to her feet. She was holding the flashlight, the beam wavering unsteadily over him, over the ground, over everything.

There was no gun.

He wanted to say something, but what? Finally, he cleared his throat.

"Are you—are you okay?"

She didn't answer.

"Addison. Please. Are you—"

"Are you done?"

He winced. "I swear, I didn't come here to hurt you."

She made a little sound. He hoped it was a snort of disbelief but it might have been the sound of her swallowing her tears.

"Addison…"

"Go away," she said wearily. "Just—just climb into your truck and—"

"I came to apologize. To tell you all the stuff I said back at *El Sueño* was—was just—"

"I don't want your apology. I don't want anything but the sight of you and that truck going away from here."

Okay. She was pushing? Only a saint wouldn't push back.

"Pretending you had a gun was pretty stupid."

"Under the circumstances," she said, "I think it was pretty smart."

She was standing straighter. Her voice had taken on strength.

The lady had balls.

"Only if you don't assume I might have had one, too."

"Why would I think such a thing?"

Jake shrugged. "Hey, this is Texas."

And, by God, she laughed. He breathed a little easier.

"You sure I didn't hurt you?"

"Only my pride. I took a course in tae kwon do years ago, when I first moved to New York. The instructor said I'd be able to fight off a mugger. Now it turns out I can't fight off a cowboy."

She was back. He had to admire her. She was one tough, resilient female.

"Nobody's called me a cowboy in years."

"Maybe that's why I couldn't fight you off."

He laughed. And he paused, struggling to find the words that had to be said next. No way could she have missed what had happened when he was on top of her.

"Ah, about what happened. When I, ah, when I had you down…"

He paused again. She didn't say anything. Heat flooded his face.

"I just want you to know that—that what happened wasn't, uh, it wasn't deliberate…"

"Did something happen?" she said coldly. "I'm afraid I didn't notice."

Wow. He hadn't expected that. Okay. She figured it was payback time. He could deal with that.

"Well," he said briskly, "if you're sure you're all right—"

"I'm fine."

"Would you like me to stay with you until you get to the house?"

She gave a snort of laughter.

He felt his face heat again, but not with embarrassment.

"You know," he said carefully, "I don't know what it's like back East but around here, people accept apologies."

"They accept them back East, too, but not from jerks."

The muscle in his jaw fluttered. Enough, he thought grimly, and he turned away from her and strode to the truck.

"Captain?"

Jake looked around.

"Next time you decide to pay me a visit, just remember there are half a dozen real guns inside that house."

"A little advice," Jake said coldly. "Don't threaten a man with a gun, real or otherwise, unless you're prepared to face the consequences."

"Advice is the last thing I need from the likes of you, Captain Wilde. You've got a nasty disposition, a hair-trigger temper and you're so full of yourself that—"

Jake marched toward her.

"You want to talk about being full of yourself, lady, try explaining that outfit you wore tonight."

Addison blinked.

"I beg your pardon?"

"Black silk, cut low. Ice-pick heels." Was he actually saying these things? He sounded like a fool but the words just kept coming. "You might as well have pinned on a sign that said, *'Hello, Wilde's Crossing. Ever seen the likes of me before?'*"

Her eyes narrowed. "Are you finished?"

Finished? Finished? No. He was not finished, nowhere near finished.

"You know," he said, "I behaved like a damned fool back at *El Sueño.*"

"If you're waiting for me to disagree—"

"But what you did here was worse."

"Worse? Defending myself against you was worse?"

"I could have killed you."

His words were flat and cold. Addison felt the chill of them straight into the marrow of her bones.

"Don't get me wrong. You were scared. A truck, following you on these dark, deserted roads…I understand that. But once you pulled that trick with your car, put your headlights on me, that flashlight, saw who I was—"

"I saw who you were, all right." For the first time since he'd taken her down, her voice quavered. "A man who wanted to—to—"

Addison shuddered. The wind was chilly; in her rush to leave *El Sueño*, she'd left her jacket behind.

"I'm not that kind of man," Jake said flatly. "Despite this face."

"Goddammit," she said with hot fury, "do you think that's what this is about? You and your face? You, feeling sorry for yourself?

Jake took a quick step forward, muscles taut with anger. "Who in hell do you think you are?"

"I'm a woman who's not afraid to tell you the truth, unlike that—that bunch of sympathy sisters at your ranch." Her chin rose; she tossed her hair back from her face. "Grow up, Captain. You were wounded. You have scars. People react to seeing them. So what?"

"You're out of line," he said coldly.

"I am very much in line. You have a chip on your shoulder the size of a house."

"You don't know a damned thing about me."

"And you don't know a damned thing about me, but that didn't stop you from making a snap judgment. And I am sick and tired of snap judgments. You got that?"

Jake hesitated. Then he nodded.

"You're right," he said in a low voice. "You want to know the truth of what happened tonight? I saw you. And I wanted you. I haven't wanted a woman in what seems like forever but one look at you and all that changed. And then—then, my brothers told me you weren't looking at me, Jacob Wilde, you were looking at me, the guy they'd recommended to check out your ranch and I, hell, and I—"

"I saw you watching me. And I told myself I was just trying to get your attention so we could talk business but—but—"

"Dammit," he said, and either she moved or he did.

It didn't matter.

What counted was that an instant later, she was in his arms.

CHAPTER SIX

THERE WAS NO time to try and understand what was happening.

This was magic, and only a fool would question it.

Jake was a lot of things, but he wasn't a fool. He was a man with a beautiful woman in his arms, her mouth warm against his.

She whispered something against his lips. Was she asking him to stop?

No.

Thank God, no, because stopping the kiss would have killed him.

If anything, he wanted more.

And she gave it, her lips parting eagerly so he could taste her hot, honeyed sweetness.

She slid her tongue against his. And moaned.

The sound went straight through him.

She went up on her toes, the flashlight tumbling to the ground.

His arms tightened around her as she wound her arms around his neck.

He could hear his blood roaring in his ears.

On a low, rough groan, he tilted her head back and took the kiss deeper.

She trembled, pressed her body more tightly to his.

The kiss went on and on; the moon and the stars spun around them. They were the center of the universe, its source of light and heat—

And the kiss wasn't enough.

Jake stumbled back against the truck and lifted Addison into him. She clung to him. He moved his hips against her and the sound she made when she felt his erection was raw with need.

Everything within him responded.

He was steel. He was granite. He was dangerously close to losing control.

"Addison," he said in a warning whisper, "Addison..."

She sank her teeth delicately into the tender flesh of his bottom lip. Rocked against him. Said his name in a hoarse whisper, and whatever remained of his sanity fled.

He hoisted her off the ground, one arm under her bottom, his free hand beneath her skirt. She wrapped her legs around him.

He sought her heat, found it, found the wetness that was for him, only for him, and cupped her with his palm.

She gave a sharp, keening cry.

"Please," she sobbed, "Jacob, Jacob, please..."

Beyond thought, beyond everything rational, he wrapped his fingers around the small bit of silk that kept him from her and tore it away.

She gasped.

Now he could feel her against his fingers.

Wet heat. Soft curls. The delicate petals of the flower that was her feminine heart.

He stroked her. She screamed. The intensity of her response almost finished him.

Quickly, he reached between them, unzipped, freed himself, lifted her higher...

And drove into her.

She clamped around him, a velvet vise.

Hold on, he told himself, *don't let go, not yet, not yet, not—*

But she kissed him. Lifted herself. Came down on his aroused flesh. Once. Twice. Again...

She screamed again. Convulsed around him.

And the cosmos whirled them away in its star-studded embrace.

* * *

His heartbeat slowed.

He felt hers slowing, too.

The sounds of the night settled around them.

So did his ability to think.

What in hell had just happened?

He'd been with a lot of women. Until the last year and a half, more, perhaps, than most men.

He'd always liked sex, liked the tastes, the textures of a woman's body, and he was no stranger to sex as a sudden, exciting encounter.

But this—

This wasn't like anything he'd ever known.

Part of him said it was because he hadn't had a woman in a long time.

Liar, a voice inside him whispered.

He'd gone without sex before, during long combat missions, even during self-imposed periods of celibacy before combat when instinct told him that self-imposed deprivation would make him stronger.

There was no explanation for what had just happened. He'd lost his self-control.

No finesse.

No tenderness.

And, sweet Jesus, no condom.

Still, he wanted to take her again. Slowly. With time to do all the things he hadn't done.

Undress her.

Taste her.

Kiss her breasts, suck on her nipples…

"Put me down."

Her voice was toneless. Even a man still trying to figure out if he'd lost his sanity could tell that wasn't a good sign.

"Listen," he said, "about this—"

"Did you hear me? Put me down."

He nodded, lowered her carefully to her feet and searched his head for something intelligent to say. Nothing happened, so he went for a time-honored classic.

"You okay?"

She didn't answer. Yeah, well, why would she? Surely, what he'd said was among the stupidest lines a man could utter.

What was she thinking? He couldn't tell, couldn't see her face. Her hair was a wild tangle, obscuring her features.

"Hey," he said softly. He scrunched down, just enough so they were at eye level, and put a hand under her chin. "Addy?"

Her head came up. "My name," she said, "is Addison."

No, Jake thought, that was definitely not a good sign, either.

"Look, I'm just trying to ask if you're—"

"I know what you're trying to ask. I'm on the pill."

He felt a sense of relief, but that hadn't really been what he was asking. He meant, had he hurt her? Disappointed her? Was she already filled with regret or, like him, did she want more?

Most of all, did she understand this any better than he did?

"Good," he said, nodding his head like one of those silly dolls you saw in the windows of cars. "Good. But what I meant was, you know—"

Hell. He was stumbling around like a boy after his first conquest. He cleared his throat and tried again.

"I know this was a little fast—"

"Such a smooth talker, Captain." She jerked away from his hand. "Besides, it's a little late to worry about that, isn't it?"

Jake's mouth thinned.

"What's that supposed to mean?"

His tone was suddenly cold. Addison couldn't blame him. He'd asked a damned good question.

What had just happened—down-and-dirty sex with a man she had just met, a man who'd accused her of trying to seduce him into bed or maybe into accepting a job—had involved the both of them.

There was no way she could blame it on Jake Wilde alone, much as she wanted to.

She'd been part of it.

Her throat constricted.

More than part.

She'd been an eager participant.

The proof was in each wild, exciting memory.

The taste of him, still on her lips.

The scent of him, still in each breath she took.

The echo of her own voice, feverishly repeating his name, asking him, begging him to—to—

Her belly knotted.

She thought of how they must look, he standing with his back to a truck in the middle of nowhere, she standing before him, what they'd just done stamped all over her.

His tie was askew.

More to the point, she didn't have her panties on.

She wanted to weep with humiliation. That

she, of all people, would do such a thing. She'd grown up with a mother whose attitude toward men had devolved to something about as complicated as her attitude toward potato chips.

Why have just one if more are available?

As for her…she wasn't a virgin. She wasn't some sad little innocent. She'd had sex before.

A few times…

Very few.

The truth was, she was on the pill to regulate her menstrual cycle, not for anything more exciting.

For one crazy second, she thought of telling him that.

And almost laughed.

What would she say? *I'm not the kind of girl who has sex up against a truck with a man I've known for five minutes….*

But she was. And there was no explanation for it that would make her feel better.

"Look," he said, his tone conciliatory, "I know you're upset…."

She took one quick look at his face, all hard angles and planes in the moonlight, and then she turned away.

The flashlight lay at their feet, still lit, the

beam illuminating—she shuddered—illuminating what remained of her panties and one shoe.

What had become of the other?

As if it mattered.

She bent. So did he. His hand closed on hers as she reached for the flashlight. She pulled her hand free, picked up the light and the scrap of silk that was proof of her shame.

"Dammit," he growled, "talk to me!"

She looked at him. The muscle in his jaw was flickering. What did he expect her to say? *Thank you for the good time?*

"Listen, lady, I'm not going to let you pretend this didn't happen."

"*You're* not going to let *me* pretend this didn't happen?" Addison tossed her tangled curls back from her eyes. "Here's a news flash, Captain. What I do or don't do isn't up to you!"

He caught her by the wrist again; she gasped as he pulled her closer. "We're a little past the 'Captain' routine. And, yeah, you're damned right, what you do is none of my business."

"I'm glad we agree," she said coldly.

The pressure on her wrist increased; he tugged her the last few inches toward him until there was virtually no space separating them at all.

"But there's no way I'm going to let you look at me as if I forced you to do this. We made love," he said bluntly. "Why can't you accept that?"

"We had sex," she snapped. "And if you don't know the difference, I feel sorry for you."

The quick change in his expression terrified her. She stared up at him. Even in her stilettos, she'd had to look up to see his face.

Now, she had to tilt her head back.

It made her feel powerless.

"Do not," he said, very softly, "do not ever make the mistake of feeling sorry for me."

His hand fell from hers. He turned on his heel, swung the Tundra's door open and climbed behind the wheel.

"And you're right, Ms. McDowell. We had sex. Nothing to write home about, either."

Addison forced a little smile. "At least we agree on something."

It was the worst kind of lie and it left the taste of ashes in her mouth, but the look he shot her told her it was a small victory.

God knew, she needed it.

Head up, shoulders back, she marched

away from him toward her car, still shoeless. No way was she going to give him the pleasure of watching her search for that miserable missing shoe.

She waited for the sound of the truck starting up.

Nothing happened.

Her spine tingled. She could feel his eyes on her. She wanted to run but she wouldn't do it.

This was her property.

He was still watching as she got behind the wheel, started the engine and turned on her lights. It wasn't far to the house, only a couple of hundred yards.

Would he follow?

Would he expect to have sex with her again?

Her heart began to race as she imagined what would happen if he came after her. If he took her not against a truck but in a bed.

Naked, skin to skin. That hard, powerful body under her hands.

He was like no one she'd ever known before. Beautiful. Proud. Complex.

And wild.

God, so wild…

She reached the house, stumbled from the truck and went to the porch.

She was alone.

His truck, engine idling, stood unmoving.

He wasn't coming after her.

Still, she didn't take an easy breath until she was inside the house with the door closed and locked. She leaned back against it, panting.

The truck roared to life. The engine faded.

Jacob Wilde was gone.

Shaken, she slumped against the door.

"Damn you," she whispered.

Tears filled her eyes. Not tears of sorrow. She had never believed in feeling sorry for herself.

It was just that after all this time, she'd behaved exactly the way the world had always seen her, first when she was a girl and an entire town seemed to hold its breath, waiting for her to become her mother's daughter, and then after Charlie's death.

What had happened with Jacob Wilde made no sense. You slept with a man after you got to know him. After you decided you liked him, had things in common. You went to dinner, to the theater; you took long walks, came home, made popcorn, watched a movie.

Addison tossed her purse and the flashlight on a small table.

Okay, so she wasn't an expert on when-to-have-sex protocol.

But she knew one thing for certain.

You didn't have sex with a stranger.

She didn't, anyway. Never mind that it had been exciting and, God, incredible; never mind that she'd never had an orgasm before and on this night, in, what, five minutes, she'd had two.

Three, she thought, and she shut her eyes, remembered the liquid, hot feeling of Jake inside her, Jake taking her up and up and up…

Her eyes popped open.

"Are you out of your mind?" she said.

She had to be.

Or maybe she was just worn out.

Losing Charlie had been painful. The whispers had been agony. And then she'd come down here and found a ranch that looked like something out of a bad dream…

"Okay," she said briskly.

Forget what had just happened.

Forget Jake Wilde.

Forget everything.

She would blank all of it from her mind. She'd blank out Texas, too, and Wilde's Crossing. She belonged in New York, where life was a lot easier to understand.

She'd had enough.

To hell with finding out exactly what the ranch was worth.

"Charlie," Addison muttered as she made her way upstairs, "forgive me, old friend, but I don't like this place one little bit."

Tomorrow, she'd contact the Realtor.

And go home.

CHAPTER SEVEN

JAKE SLEPT badly.

The truth was, he hardly slept at all but there was nothing new in that. He spent most nights tossing and turning, only to fall asleep and dream things that made him wake with his heart pounding, his skin drenched in sweat.

At least last night's dreams had been different, he thought as he stood in the shower and let the water sluice down over him.

They hadn't been nightmares about firefights and IEDs and men dying because he hadn't been able to save them.

Last night's dreams had been about the feel of a woman's skin. The taste of her mouth. The scent of her hair.

The dreams had been about Addison, how it had felt to make love to her....

Jake frowned, shut off the water and reached for a towel.

Not love.

Sex.

She'd been right about that, and so what? There was no reason to disguise a basic human need with layers of phony hearts and flowers.

It was her attitude that ticked him off.

They'd had good sex. Hell, he thought, knotting the towel around his hips and glaring at his face in the mirror, they'd had great sex.

The problem was, when it was over, she'd acted as if what had happened was ugly. As if he'd somehow forced himself on her, or coerced her into giving in to him.

"No way," he muttered as he lathered his face and reached for his razor.

She'd been a willing participant.

More than willing, he thought, remembering the way she'd wrapped herself around him, her moans, her cries, her wetness and heat….

His hand slipped. The blade bit at his flesh. A tiny dot of blood appeared high on his cheek.

He cursed, tore off a square of toilet tissue and dabbed at it.

It was true, though.

She'd been with him all the way. Clinging to him. Riding him. Kissing him, biting his lip…

"Dammit, Wilde…"

He was turning himself on. And wasn't that interesting, for lack of a better word?

He hadn't had an erection since he'd been wounded, even though the docs had assured him that his equipment still worked. Now, just remembering what he'd done with a woman he didn't even like was giving him a hard-on.

What he needed, he thought coldly, was a trip to Dallas, a night at a singles bar where either some hot-looking babe with enough booze in her to ignore the face staring back at him from the mirror or one who'd find his face a turn-on would take him home to bed.

Did that explain last night? Was the McDowell woman the kind who saw something interesting in a man who was disfigured?

It didn't matter.

His hormones were working again. They'd told him that would happen. It didn't have a thing to do with her except that she'd been in the right place at the right time.

Jake splashed cool water on his face, tossed the towel aside and stepped back into his bedroom. His clothes were still in the closet and dresser, same as they had been when he first left for the army. He pulled on faded jeans. An equally faded chambray shirt. A pair of roper boots, the leather worn soft and pliable with age.

No need to wear his uniform anymore.

His time in the service was over. So was his life here, working the ranch. He'd loved both things, always figured one or the other would become his career.

Not anymore.

He needed a fresh start. Where, doing what… He had no idea. All he knew was that he was going in search of the answers.

Last night, he'd figured on heading out right away but another day wouldn't matter. He wanted to spend a little time with his family.

He ran his hands through his damp hair, tucked his wallet and keys in his pockets, put the patch over his eye. A glance out the window revealed a pewter sky, ripe with the portents of rain.

A deep breath.

Then he grabbed a denim jacket, opened the bedroom door and went in search of coffee.

The Wildes were gathered in the kitchen.

The girls were at the stove, an amazing

sight in itself because Lissa was the only cook among them and she usually shooed her sisters away.

Today, Emma was scrambling eggs, Lissa was taking a pan of biscuits from the oven and Jaimie was frying bacon.

Travis and Caleb were sitting at the big oak table that was the heart of the kitchen, sipping coffee and reading the newspaper.

For a minute, he stood and watched them, these people he loved and who loved him.

He'd let them down.

That was the worst part.

They didn't know it but he had—and why in hell hadn't he stepped off that plane last night, gone straight to the ticket counter and booked himself to L.A. or New York or Seattle or—

"Hey," Travis said, "it lives!"

Caleb grinned. "Had a late night, did you, my man?"

Jake searched for an answer. Foolish, when all he had to do was grin back and say nothing.

Somehow, he couldn't.

Em unknowingly came to his rescue with a mug of black coffee, a one-armed hug and a smacking kiss.

"Sit down, little brother, and pay no attention to these jerks."

Little brother. She'd always called him that because he was the youngest of the Wilde brothers, even though he had four years on her as well as seven or eight inches.

"Do I ever?" he said, flashing her a smile.

Travis raised an eyebrow. "We hope you did last night."

Lissa scooped bacon and eggs on a plate, put the plate in front of Jake and hugged him, too.

"Eat while it's hot, and they hope you did what?"

Caleb shot Travis a look. "Oh, Jake said he wanted to get some air, so we told him to take Trav's truck and go for a drive."

Jaimie put the basket of biscuits on the table, dropped a kiss on Jake's head, sat next to him and said, "A drive where?"

Jake looked at the food. The coffee was all he wanted—he had the feeling anything else would lodge in his throat—but his sisters would never let him get away with that, especially when it was obvious they'd shooed away Senora Lopez, the housekeeper, so they could make breakfast themselves.

"Believe it or not," Caleb said in a deliberate stage-whisper, "it's all edible,"

Em grabbed a napkin and threw it at him. "A drive where?" she said.

Jake concentrated on forking up some eggs. "Oh, you know. Just around."

Jaimie ruffled his hair. "We wondered what happened to you."

Lissa nodded. "We thought it might have something to do with the McDowell woman."

Jake shot his brothers a look. Travis gave a little shake of his head; Caleb mouthed a quick *no.*

"Why would you think that?"

"Well, you both vanished."

"Pretty much at the same time," Em added.

"Except, she didn't exactly vanish." Jaimie stole a strip of bacon from Jake's plate. "Ellen Boorman said she made a scene and stalked out in a huff. Anybody know what happened?"

"No," Travis and Caleb said, with one voice.

"Ellen said you were part of the scene and then you disappeared, too. So we thought you might have gone after her."

His three sisters fixed him with laserlike stares. Jake coughed.

"Piece of biscuit," he gasped. "Caught in my throat."

Em rose, went to the sink, returned with a tall glass of water. Jake nodded and gulped down half.

"So, what happened?"

"Nothing," he said quickly.

"You're not going to do an assessment for her?"

Jake narrowed his eyes at his brothers, who looked at each other then gave their complete attention to their mugs of coffee.

"Where'd you hear that?"

Lissa shrugged. "Around," she said airily. "Are you?"

"No. I'm not."

"Because?"

"Because," he said, putting down his knife and fork, "because I'm not—I'm not—"

"Not what?" Em asked, and that was when he remembered he'd still not told his sisters he wasn't staying.

"Because he won't have the time," Jaimie said blithely, "once he's taken up his duties here."

Silence fell over the room.

"Jeez, Jaimie," Caleb said.

Jaimie held up her hands. "What'd I do?"

"What duties?" Jake said carefully.

Travis sighed.

"Well, running *El Sueño.* Taking it over. You know."

Jake narrowed his gaze.

"No, I don't know. You want to tell me what you're talking about?"

Caleb gave an elaborate shrug.

"Tom Sloane is retiring. Remember?"

"Of course I remember. What does this have to do with me?"

"Well, the General thinks—"

"The General thinks," Jake repeated slowly.

"So do we. All of us. We hoped you'd step into Tom's shoes. More than that, actually. We're all part owners of The Dream, of course, but we want you to be its CEO."

"The paperwork is all drawn up," Lissa said.

Caleb and Travis groaned.

"Paperwork?" Jake said carefully.

"Legal documents. Changes to the trust that holds *El Sueño*, that will reflect you taking over operations."

Jake looked at his brothers.

"You went ahead and did this even though I told you that I'm not staying."

"Oh, Jake," Em said. Her sisters shushed her.

"Well, we were hoping you changed your mind."

"Didn't it occur to you to consult me?"

"Sure. But—"

Jake was angry. Angrier than the situation demanded. He knew that—but knowing it didn't change a thing.

He shoved back his chair, tossed his napkin on the table and got to his feet.

"How nice of you all to plan out my life."

"Hey, man, we aren't—"

"Yeah. You are."

"Look, *El Sueño* needs you. And you need *El Sueño.*"

And there it was. The cause of his anger. Jake leaned over, slapped his palms flat against the tabletop.

"What am I, the family rehab project?"

"Jake," Travis said, "we love you."

"Then don't play at being my therapists," he said, and he ignored his sisters' voices calling after him and got out of the house before he said something he'd truly regret.

His car was where he'd left it last night.

Enough of this, he thought as he got behind the wheel. He had no idea what he wanted to do with his life but one thing was certain.

He wasn't going to let anyone make his decisions for him.

Not anymore, he told himself grimly as he started the car and got moving.

He should have taken off first thing that morning.

He hadn't wanted to hurt his sisters. And, dammit, that was exactly what he'd do, if he left now.

He thought about seeking out Travis and Caleb and telling them it was time they learned to mind their own business but he knew what they'd said was true.

They loved him.

And they were worried about him. That was why they'd come up with the half-baked idea of him running the ranch.

The entire Wilde clan had decided he was depressed or suffering from PTSD when, in truth, post-traumatic stress disorder was not the problem.

The problem was, he was a failure.

It started to rain as he turned onto the county highway.

Great. Rain certainly suited his mood.

Had Caleb or Travis told Addison McDowell he needed a reason to feel useful?

Had they asked her to take pity on him?

His jaw tightened.

Was pity at the heart of what had happened last night?

The possibility made him sick. And angry.

There was only one way to get an answer.

Jake pulled onto the shoulder of the road, made a U-turn and headed for the Chambers ranch.

He drove fast and hard, and reached the ranch in half the time it normally would have taken.

His anger was still boiling when he pulled up outside the house.

The rain beat down on him as he got out of the car and slammed the door shut. Scowling, he turned up the collar of his jacket, stalked up the sagging wooden steps to the porch and jabbed at the bell.

Silence.

"Dammit," he muttered, and banged his fist against the door.

Nothing.

She had to be inside.

Her car—he could see that it was a plain vanilla rental Chevy—was parked where he'd seen her leave it. In the glow of his headlights, he'd seen her get out of it and rush inside the house as if the hounds of hell were at her heels.

Had she been afraid of him?

Was she tucked away inside, afraid of him now?

Jake stuck his hands in his pockets, looked down at his boots.

He wouldn't blame her if she were. He'd behaved like a crazy man and here he was this morning, stomping across her porch, banging on her door….

And why in hell would he think she'd made love with him out of pity? Had sex with him, whatever she wanted to call it?

She'd been as carried away as he'd been.

No matter how things had ended, she deserved better than those cold and ugly thoughts.

Enough, he thought, and he trotted down the steps, got back into his car and drove away.

Addison watched from an upstairs window as Jacob Wilde drove off.

Good. In fact, excellent.

The last thing she wanted was to deal with him this morning.

She was busy getting things in order inside this—this catastrophe of a house.

Despite her best intentions, she wasn't going to be able to leave today. There wasn't a seat on a New York-bound flight out of Dallas until the end of the week.

Not a problem.

She wasn't fleeing Wilde's Crossing, she was simply heading home.

There was plenty to keep her occupied for a few days.

Like what she was about to tackle. Emptying a hall closet on the second floor.

"Yuck," she muttered.

It wouldn't be fun, but it had to be done.

Over the weeks, she'd cleaned all the rooms, scrubbed the kitchen and ancient bathroom. She'd even done some touch-ups—polished the floor, painted the walls, bought some odds and ends for the biggest bedroom, which was the one she slept in.

She'd done the closet there but nowhere else, and she had not even looked at the attic.

She could put the house on the market as it was, but for all she knew, there was a treasure trove of interesting old stuff right here, under her nose.

Checking would be fun—

Okay.

Addison stepped away from the closet, sighed and sank down, cross-legged, on the floor.

Maybe not.

She'd probably find nothing but spiders and dust. Still, it would give her something to do instead of thinking about last night.

Thinking about it was pretty much all she'd managed this morning.

That man. Jake Wilde.

"Such arrogance," she told the empty room.

Indeed.

Arrogance. Audacity. Ego.

The nerve of him to show up here today.

Why had he come?

She couldn't think of a reason, unless he thought he could talk her into a repeat performance.

No. That hadn't been it.

A man hoping to take a woman to bed wouldn't have looked so damned angry.

As if he had anything to be angry about when she was the one who—

Addison froze.

What was that? A car?

Frowning, she rose, went into the closest bedroom and drew back a corner of the curtain.

Jake Wilde's car.

He was back.

The man was persistent, if nothing else.

Jake stood on the porch and rang the bell.

Knocked on the door. Knocked, not banged. No answer, so he switched to ringing the bell again.

Eventually, he heard a window slide open somewhere above him. He took a step back, looked up, saw Addison, her face half-obscured by a flapping lace curtain the color of old gym socks.

He took a breath, let it out, cleared his throat.

"Ms. McDowell." Did you address a woman so formally after you'd slept with her? But he hadn't slept with her. He'd all but screwed out his brains and hers against a truck…and, hell, that kind of image didn't belong in his head right now. "Addison," he said pleasantly, "good—"

"You have ten seconds to turn around and get off my land, Captain. After that, I call the police."

So much for being pleasant.

"Take it easy, okay? You don't need the police."

"I'll decide what I need. The police, the FBI, the National Guard. How about the cavalry?"

"Look, I just want to talk to you."

"You have nothing to say that I want to hear."

"How do you know until I say it?"

"When I was in college, I took a class in Platonic dialectic. I'm not going to get dragged into this discussion."

Jake raised an eyebrow. "I took a class in contract negotiation. Does that make us even?"

It was difficult not to laugh. He was quick, and he was funny.

As if either thing mattered.

"Here's the bottom line," Addison said. "We have nothing to talk about."

"What about last night?"

"What about it?"

"We need to talk about that."

"We already did."

She was right; they had. And the excuse he'd given himself when he'd been here fifteen minutes ago wasn't valid, either.

He hadn't come to confront her.

He'd come because he just plain wanted to see her.

What if he told her that?

"Captain?"

Jake nodded. Looked up. "I'm still here."

"And I've just proved that there's no purpose to your visit. So do us both a favor. Go away."

"I probably should."

"There's no 'probably' about it."

"I would, if I were smart."

"Yay," she said, and he tried not to laugh when he heard her clapping her hands together.

"But I'm not smart. If I were, I'd have done the right thing last night."

"What did I say? I do not want to talk about—"

"I'd have told you," he said gruffly, "that I wasn't sorry we'd made love—"

"Goodbye, Captain."

"—because," he said quickly, before she could close the window, "because the truth is, I wanted you more than I've ever wanted a woman. And what we did..." His smile was slow and intimate and she could feel it, straight into the marrow of her bones. "What we did," he said, "was fantastic."

Addison stared at the man looking up at her from the porch.

What did she say to that blunt admission?

That blunt, incredibly sexy admission?

The man was a puzzle. He confused the hell out of her.

Just looking at him was confusing.

No uniform today. Instead, he was dressed like a, well, a cowboy. Faded shirt. Faded jeans. Boots that she could tell had nothing to do with style. Even here, in the heart of ranching country, she'd seen a lot of that. Style, no substance.

And, of course, he was wearing that eye patch, hiding what the war had done to him from the world.

He looked—there was that word again—beautiful. And so masculine she was finding it difficult to remember how much she despised him.

It was quite a combination. Arrogance and vulnerability in one gorgeous package…

She'd never known a man like him. And the sex—*the sex*, she thought, almost hearing the italics in her head—as for that…

Why lie to herself?

It had been…there had to be a better word than *fantastic*.

Sex was okay. But it wasn't mind-blowing.

Until last night. Until he'd taken her in his arms. Was that why she'd heaped all the blame on him? Because it was less embarrassing than the truth?

Those moments when he'd been inside her, when their mouths and bodies had been fused…

"Okay."

Addison came back to reality. Jake was still looking at her but he'd gone down the steps, even backed up a couple of feet.

Now that he had, she could see that he had a bouquet of flowers in his arms.

"You don't want to talk to me," he said, "I guess I can't blame—"

The window sash fell into place. The dishwater-gray curtain swung back to cover the glass.

He put the bouquet down on the porch. Then he tucked his hands into his back pockets and headed for his car.

And felt a moment of ineffable loss, and wasn't that ridiculous? He'd apologized. She'd refused the apology. End of—

"Hey."

Her voice was soft but it stopped him in

his tracks. He turned and saw her in the open doorway.

His gaze swept over her.

No black silk dress.

No stilettos.

She wore oversize gray sweats. Her feet were bare. Her hair hung loose around her face, a shining curve of darkness.

Something seemed to turn over inside him.

As beautiful as she'd been last night, she was even more beautiful now.

The sight of her made him wish they could start over, even though all they'd have was today.

She cleared her throat.

"I was just going to make some fresh coffee. Would you…would like some, Captain?"

Jake looked at her for what seemed forever.

"It's Jake," he said gruffly. "And coffee sounds…it sounds great. Thanks."

He retrieved the bouquet. She took a step back as he climbed the porch steps. When he reached her, she felt her pulse leap.

"Actually," she said, "actually, it really won't be great. The coffee, I mean. The pot I found in the kitchen is—is just about as—as antiquated as the rest of the—the rest of the—"

"Addison."

The way he spoke her name, the way he was looking at her, told her everything she wanted to know, including the fact that coffee was the last thing on his mind.

Or hers.

"Jacob," she whispered, and he dropped the flowers as she stepped into his arms.

CHAPTER EIGHT

JAKE KICKED the door shut behind him.

The interior of the house was dark and cool; the silence of the empty rooms was all around them. There was a scent in the air—her scent. The scent of flowers he hadn't been able to define.

"Addison," he said softly.

She turned her face up to his. Her eyes filled with him, and a rush of something primitive and possessive swept through him.

"Be sure," he said in a rough whisper as he tunneled his fingers into the silken darkness of her hair. "Because once we start—"

She rose to him and pressed her lips to his.

"Make love to me, Jacob," she said.

Jake groaned, drew her hard against him and claimed her mouth with a deep, possessive kiss.

Just that quickly, last night's hunger blazed

inside him again. His big body shuddered; his blood beat hot and heavy in his ears. The driving need to make Addison his was all that mattered….

No.

She was all that mattered.

He wanted more than her body.

He wanted her.

In bed. Naked. Her dark hair spread over the pillows.

He wanted her needing his touch, pleading for it, as desperate for him as he was for her.

Teeth gritted, fighting hard for control, he caught her up in his arms.

"Hold on to me," he whispered.

She wrapped her arms around his neck. Buried her face against his throat. He could feel her heart thundering against his, her breath on his skin.

The stairs were just ahead. Another couple of minutes, he told himself as he climbed them.

He could last that long.

Only one door was open on the second floor. Jake shouldered his way past it. He knew this old house, its gray rooms and dark walls, but this room—Addison's room, without question—had been transformed.

Polished wood floor. Shiny brass bed. Brick fireplace, neatly stacked with wood. White walls, white curtains, white bed linens and duvet—and the faintly mingled scent of flowers and fresh paint.

The room was a reflection of her.

Honest. Elegant. Beautiful.

He lowered her to her feet beside the bed, did it slowly so she could feel how hard and ready he was, so he could feel all her lovely, soft curves.

She was trembling.

"Don't be afraid," he said in a gruff whisper. "This will be different, I swear it."

Her eyes, pools of liquid silver, lifted to his. "I'm not afraid. Not of you, Jacob, never of—"

He kissed her. Parted her lips with his. Feasted on the exquisite taste of her.

She caught his collar in her hands, lifted herself to him, sucked the tip of his tongue into the heat of her mouth.

He groaned with pleasure.

His hands cupped her breasts. He could feel her nipples tightening, lifting even through the heavy cotton of her shirt. Groaning, he slipped his hands under it.

Ah, God!

She was naked. No bra. Nothing between his calloused fingers and the silk and satin of her skin.

"Jacob," she whispered. "Jacob, please…"

The one word, so filled with need, almost took him to his knees. He pushed up the sweatshirt, bent to her, sucked at her nipples, pressed them against the roof of his mouth with his tongue.

She tasted of cream and honey.

"You are so beautiful," he said thickly. "So very beautiful…"

His thumbs rolled over her nipples. She moaned; he watched her face as he caressed her, saw her eyes go dark with pleasure.

Sweat beaded his forehead as he tugged her sweatshirt over her head and tossed it aside.

He could see her breasts more clearly now. They were high, rounded, just right for his mouth and his hands.

He kissed them. The curves, the slopes, the apricot nipples. He couldn't get enough of their silky feel, their delicate flavor; he couldn't get enough of watching her face as he brought her closer and closer to orgasm from this, just from this.

She began undoing the buttons of his shirt.

He helped her. Then he swore softly and the remaining buttons went flying.

His shirt landed on the floor, and she went into his arms.

Skin against skin.

Heat against heat.

He knew he couldn't last much longer.

He drew back. Hooked his thumbs into the sides of her sweatpants, pushed them down…

And went still.

She was wearing panties.

White cotton this time, not lace. They were simple, innocent, dotted with tiny blue flowers.

An equally tiny blue bow rode just below each hip bone.

Jake went to his knees.

Kissed her belly. Her navel. The little blue bows.

And drew the panties down, down, down.

They pooled at her ankles. He cupped her hips with his hands. Brought his face closer.

She gasped.

"Wait," she said in a shaky whisper. "Really, I don't think—"

He put his mouth against her, at the apex of her thighs. Her dark curls were silken against his lips.

"Open for me," he said thickly, and she shifted her legs, shifted again...

And screamed in ecstasy when he found her with his mouth and tongue.

She tasted of passion and of woman, and when he licked at her, her cries rose into the stillness of the morning.

Jake got to his feet, kicked off his boots and jeans and took her down onto the bed with him.

He caught a fistful of her hair. Bent to her. Kissed her. He couldn't stop kissing her, couldn't get enough of that soft, sweet mouth.

Her hands were on him.

Cool. Soft. They swept over his back, his chest; they framed his face as she lifted herself to him and kissed him.

"Addison," he said, and she said yes, oh, yes, and he moved over her, knelt between her thighs, slid his hands under her...

"Look at me," he demanded.

Her eyes went to his face.

And he entered her.

She moaned.

His breath caught.

She was wet and hot, tight as a silk fist closing around him as he went deeper, deeper...

She cried out his name. He was shaking.

But, somehow, he held himself still.

Waited until her muscles took all of him in.

Then, slowly, he drew back. Not all the way. Just enough. The sensation, so exquisite, so exciting, made him shudder.

She went wild beneath him.

He caught hold of her hands, brought them to her sides, moved faster, faster…

"Jacob."

Her voice was low. Breathless. She said his name again and lifted to his thrusts, her body an arcing bow of pleasure as his arrowed into her.

The world blurred.

Sweat glistened on his skin.

"Now," he said, and she came, sobbing his name, her legs locked around him, her hands clutching his shoulders.

He gave one long, rough groan.

Then he flew with her into a rainbow of color and light.

He lay sprawled over her.

His body was solid. Hard. He outweighed her by who knew how many dozen pounds.

His weight pinned her to the mattress….

And, oh, it was a lovely feeling.

When he moved, she gave a little *mmm* of protest.

"I'm too heavy for you," he whispered.

"No," she whispered back. "You're not."

She felt his lips curve against her throat.

"I am," he said.

She sighed. "I don't care."

No. Neither did he. He could stay exactly where he was, forever.

Still, after a minute or two, he rolled off her, wrapped her in his arms, drew her against him so that her head was on his shoulder and kissed her.

A pleased sigh eased from her lips. She felt his mouth curve against hers in response.

"Yeah," he said, his voice low, a little hoarse. "I think so, too."

Was sex supposed to be like this?

She couldn't ask him; no way would she expose her ignorance but the truth was that even though she had a reputation that would have given Salome a run for her money, this was all new.

She'd had only three prior lovers. One had been a virgin, like her. It had happened in college. The other two had been when she was in law school.

Nice guys, all of them.

But the sex…

It hadn't been memorable.

This—this experience with Jacob… Okay. Both experiences with Jacob…

Memorable.

Incredibly memorable.

Although today might even have been better, Addison thought, repressing a little shiver of delight.

For one thing, the rain had stopped. Daylight was streaming through the windows.

She could see Jacob.

He could see her.

She tried not to blush at the thought.

Plus, last night, escaping his arms, putting space between them, had been what she'd longed for.

Not today.

She wanted to lie here forever. Just like this. Her head pillowed on his shoulder. With his hand stroking the length of her body.

He was doing it in a way that sent just the tips of his fingers over her breast, over her nipple…

She *was* blushing now. She could feel the rise of heat in her face.

And he knew it. Just look at how he was grinning.

"Whatever you're thinking," he said, "how about sharing it with me?"

"That was..." She cleared her throat. "It was...nice."

"Nice? *Nice?*" He scowled, rose up on one elbow and looked down at her. "You know how to hurt a guy, McDowell."

He was teasing her. And she loved it.

Who'd have thought sex could involve laughter?

He grinned. Rolled her on her back. Caught her wrists, pinned her hands high over her head.

"Admit it."

Oh, the feel of him against her. All that hard, lean muscle...

"Admit what?" she said breathlessly.

"Admit this was better than nice."

"Maybe," she said, teasing him back.

"Maybe, the woman says." He shifted a little. She bit back a moan. He was becoming aroused. She could feel him against her belly.

"Lots better than nice," he said in a low, sexy whisper.

She wanted to say something clever, but all she could manage was a soft moan.

He kissed her mouth. She returned the kiss.

He moved. She did, too.

The engorged head of his erection was between her thighs. It brushed against her sensitized flesh.

"Please," she said.

"Please, what?" he said, and then he was inside her, moving inside her, and the world tilted and spun away.

This time, after he withdrew, he wrapped them both in the duvet.

Then he drew her into the warm shelter of his arms and kissed her temple.

"Sleep," he said softly.

She couldn't. She was lying on her right side, and she never—she never—

When she woke, there were long shadows in the room, and a fire leaping in the hearth.

Jake, wearing only his jeans, squatted beside it, feeding wood to the flames.

Addison sat up, the duvet clutched to her chin.

He looked around, smiled when he saw her.

"Hey," he said softly.

She shoved her hair back from her face.

"What time—" Her voice was hoarse. She cleared her throat, started again. "What time is it?"

He looked at his watch.

"Almost five."

Her eyes widened. "Almost…"

Jake rose. His beauty made her heartbeat quicken. His skin was tanned, his muscles the kind a man got from hard work, not from a gym. His jeans were zipped but unbuttoned; she couldn't keep her gaze from going to the arrow of dark, silky hair that disappeared behind his fly.

"Don't tell me," he said, as he came slowly toward her. "You have an appointment with a can of paint."

"A can of…" She laughed. "You can still smell it."

"Uh-huh." He sat down next to her, leaned in, gave her a long, lingering kiss. "You painted this room all by yourself?"

"I'm a painting expert. Do you have any idea what painters charge in New York?"

"A frugal woman." He clapped a hand to his chest. "Be still, my heart."

"A broke woman. Tuition loans. A condo mortgage."

"According to Caleb, all lawyers are rich."

"I'm an indentured servant, in my second year at Kalich, Kalich and Kalich."

He grinned. "An imaginative name for a law firm."

"Especially," Addison said, "when you consider that the last Kalich toddled off this mortal plane twenty years ago."

Jake laughed, leaned in and kissed her again. This time, she sighed and sank into the kiss.

"So," he said, curving a hand around the side of her face, "you went to Home Depot—"

"Sears. They had paint and stuff for the floor and all the other things I needed."

He shook his head. "Old man Chambers would be horrified."

"Horrified? That I cleaned up this—this—"

She was indignant. Jake tried not to laugh.

"Keeping the place a disaster area was a point of pride with him. The summers I worked here, I used to offer to deal with more than the fences and the horses. He'd always get this look on his face and tell me to mind my own business." He shrugged. "But I don't think he really let it all go to hell until the last few years, while I was…away."

Away. Addison looked at him. *Away* seemed a strange way to describe being in a war, getting wounded, doing something heroic enough to win an important medal.

"How long were you *away*?" she said softly.

A muscled knotted in his jaw.

"Too long," he said, after a minute. "And maybe not long enough."

He turned away from her…and her breath caught. A series of vicious scars pocked his right shoulder. Without thinking, she reached out and touched her fingers gently to the raw-looking flesh.

He jerked back, grabbed his shirt from the floor, shrugged it on and reached for his jeans.

"Oh, Jake, I'm sorry. Did I hurt—"

"I'm fine."

Addison reached out to him but his posture was unyielding. Instinct warned her not to touch him.

"I didn't mean to—"

"I just don't want to talk about it." His words were clipped as he rose to his feet. "I'm going to make coffee."

"Jacob. Wait—"

"I said I don't want to talk about it, okay? Go on. Get dressed."

Moments ago, they'd been part of each other. Now…

Now, she grabbed the duvet and dragged it to her chin.

She was entirely naked. Not just her body. Her soul. Her heart. In less than twenty-four hours, she'd become terrifyingly vulnerable, something she had spent most of her life avoiding.

She must have made a sound. A whimper. Something, because he swung toward her.

"Goddammit," he said. "Honey, I'm sorry."

She shook her head without looking at him. "No. No, that's okay. I just—I just—"

Jake cursed, strode back to her and gathered her tightly into his arms.

"It isn't you. It's me, honey. I don't talk about it. What happened. I don't talk about it to anybody."

She nodded. "I understand."

He almost laughed.

She didn't. She couldn't. Hell, he didn't understand it, and he lived with it.

"I flew Blackhawks," he said. "Do you know what they are?"

"Helicopters?"

"Yeah. Big, bad birds. They can carry damned near anything to a battlefield. Troops. Equipment. Anything." His voice roughened. "And they can carry things off a battlefield. They can do medical evacuations, provide cover and get men who've been pinned down, men who are dying, out of harm's way."

"Jacob, don't." She put her fingers lightly over his mouth. "You don't have to—"

"Sometimes things went right. I was lucky. Sometimes, I wasn't." His mouth twisted. "After a while, you start keeping score, you know? Two saved. Two lost. Two bastards taken out, permanently. That kind of thing."

"It must be awful. To lose men. To have to wonder what will happen next."

"Yeah. But, like I say, you keep count. As long as your numbers stay ahead, you stay sane." He paused. "And then," he said, in a low voice, "then, one day..." He shuddered. "I can't talk about it. Just—just leave it alone."

"Whatever you want," she said softly.

He stared at her while the seconds swept past. Then he groaned and wrapped her in his arms.

They sat that way for a long time. The fire in the brick hearth burned down to cinders.

Finally, Jake sighed.

"That's more than I've ever told anyone," he said softly.

He hadn't told her anything, not really, but she knew what he meant. He'd let her see beyond his wounds, to his pain.

"So," he said, and she could see how hard he was searching for something to lighten the moment, "so, one confession deserves another."

She smiled. "You think?"

"I know." He smiled, too; the smile was almost real but it still had a way to go. "For instance...it's late, we haven't eaten all day. So, I'll let you in on a Wilde secret."

She sat back and widened her eyes.

"You turn into a werewolf at midnight."

He laughed.

"I know how to cook."

Addison clapped her hand to her chest.

"Be still, my heart."

"Just tell me what you want for breakfast, or lunch, or whatever in heck this meal is, and I'll go down to the kitchen and put it together."

"Hmm. How about pancakes?"

"How about Jake Wilde's famous scrambled eggs and onions? Or Jake Wilde's dee-licious fried cheese sandwiches? See, the real confession is that I can cook, but only those two things."

She laughed.

"Okay, your turn. You have to confess something to me."

You're wonderful, she thought, but she didn't have the courage. Besides, she knew it had to be something that would make him laugh.

"My name isn't Addison."

Jake touched the tip of her nose with his finger.

"No?"

She shook her head. "No."

"Huh. What is it, then? And how come you changed it?"

"If I were to tell you what it is, you'd understand why I changed it."

"What's this 'if' stuff, McDowell? You're supposed to be telling me something here, not just telling me your name isn't Addison."

"My lips are sealed."

"They are, huh?" His smile turned masculine and sexy; he pushed her back on the bed and kissed her mouth. "Well," he said softly, "I guess I'll just have to find a way to unseal them."

She let him do just that. Then she smiled and linked her hands behind his neck.

"Okay. You've worked your magic. Bend down so I can whisper my secret."

Jake complied. He put his ear against her lips…and, suddenly, what she was about to tell him didn't seem so funny anymore.

Nobody knew her real name. Why would she admit it to him?

"You don't have to tell me," he said.

"No?"

"No. Because I figured it out. Your real name is Rumpelstiltskin."

That did it. She laughed. And said, "My name is Adoré."

Jake didn't laugh.

"Adoré," he said softly. "Adoré," he said again, as he gathered her to him. "It's a beautiful name, sweetheart. Almost as beautiful as you."

She blushed.

"You think?" she said with girlish delight, and he tumbled her back against the pillows.

"What I think," he said gruffly, "is that food can wait."

"What am I going to do with you, Jacob Wilde?"

Jake bent his head, tongued a tender pink nipple. Addison's laugh became a gasp of pleasure.

"I'll help you think of something," he whispered.

And he did.

CHAPTER NINE

ADDISON STOOD in the kitchen, wearing a robe that came down to her ankles, and stared blankly at the old clock ticking away above the stove.

"Midnight?" she said. "It can't be midnight!"

Jake, dressed only in jeans that rode low on his hips, stood leaning against the door frame, arms folded, bare feet crossed.

She was a delectable sight, and all he could think about was taking her back to bed.

But it was late, they were both hungry, and grabbing a bite to eat seemed a smart thing to do when he had every reason to keep up his energy.

The night wasn't over yet.

She looked at him. "What does your watch say?"

He looked at his watch, then at her.

"The little hand's on the twelve," he said,

deadpan. "So's the big hand. Where I come from, that means it's either midnight or high noon, honey, and considering the fact that it's pitch-black outside, my best guess is midnight."

"Midnight. I just don't see how—"

She bit her lip. And she blushed.

Damn, he loved that about her! Hours in his arms, hours spent exploring each other, and she could still turn pink as a schoolgirl.

And yet, she had all the confidence a man could want in a woman, in bed or out. You'd never be able to take her for granted; she'd always be an exciting challenge.

You could build a future with a woman like Addison McDowell.

Jake frowned.

What kind of nonsense was that? This was about terrific sex with a terrific woman. End of story.

"You're right," he said, taking things back to where they belonged. "Where could the hours have gone?"

The color in her lovely face deepened. Jake relented, straightened to his full height, walked slowly toward her and took her in his arms.

"Either we get some food in our bellies or

they're gonna find just two piles of bones on old man Chambers's magnificent linoleum floor."

Addison leaned back in his arms.

"Not a fan of linoleum, huh?"

"Frankly, I can't tell linoleum from marble. Well, yeah, I can, but it's that shade of green makes my stomach lurch."

"It's called chartreuse."

"Even worse."

She slid her hands up his naked chest, loving the feel of his skin, the silkiness of the dark hair across his sternum, the strong beat of his heart.

"We had linoleum in the kitchen when I was growing up. Not green. Pink. We had pink everything. Walls. Rugs. Bathroom." She smiled up at him. "But I got even. Every single thing in my apartment, walls to floors to furniture, is white."

"Aha."

"Aha, what?"

"Aha, that explains old man Chambers's bedroom."

"My bedroom," she said softly.

"Damned right," Jake said, his voice a little rough.

Addison locked her hands at the nape of

his neck. She could feel the very edge of his scar under the tips of her fingers. She wanted to slip behind him, press her lips to the scar, but she knew better.

Jake hadn't mentioned it again.

Still, she knew it was some kind of concession that he hadn't put on his shirt when they finally left the bed, especially since he had not once removed the black patch from his eye.

He was hurting. Not outside. He was hurting inside and she hurt for him. It was a helpless feeling, not to be able to do anything to help.

"Such deep thoughts," he said, brushing his mouth gently over hers.

Somehow, she managed a quick smile..

"Chartreuse linoleum will do that every time."

"I agree. So, how about we eat something fast so we can get out of this room just as fast?"

"A brilliant plan, Captain. What would you like?"

He gave a soft, sexy laugh. She blushed again and he drew her even closer and kissed her.

"I'm serious, Jacob."

"So am I," he said, and kissed her again.

The kiss went on for a long, lovely time. Then Addison stepped out of his arms and opened the fridge.

"Let's see—I have some cheese…."

"Excellent. I'll make us those fried cheese sandwiches." When she looked over her shoulder at him, he raised his eyebrows. "What?" he said innocently. "You're not in the mood for fried cheese?"

"Tell me you made that up."

"It's an old Wilde recipe."

"I bet your sisters would disagree."

"Well, okay, it's an old Wilde Bunch recipe."

She laughed. "You, Caleb and Travis? The Wilde Bunch, huh?"

"That's what th… Jake tucked his hands i… jeans and admired… dison's backside… shelf. "Although… is Trav's specia…

"Thank goo… said, pushing… aside.

"Mine's fr…

That brou…

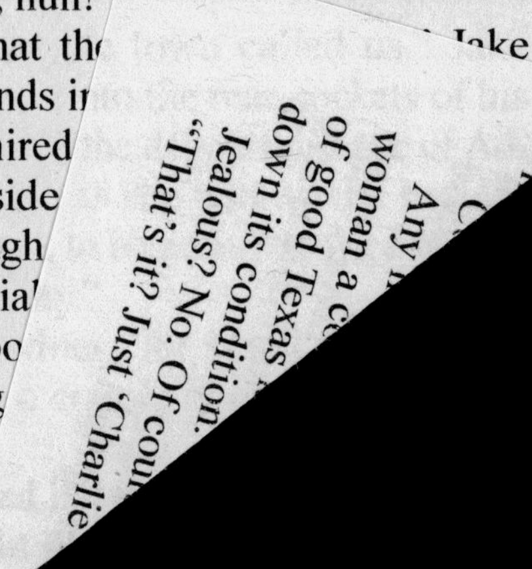

"Please tell me you're joking."

"You northerners are so judgmental."

"I'm afraid to ask what Caleb contributes to these feasts."

"Marshmallows. Not fried," he added quickly. "Charred. You know. In a fire. Crispy on the outside, melted on the inside."

"Actually, I don't know."

"What? You never sat around a campfire and toasted marshmallows?"

"Nope."

"Ah, honey," Jake said, with genuine regret, "you missed a lot."

"Charlie used to say the same thing." And even as she asked herself why she'd mentioned Charlie, the answer came to her.

It was time to know how Jake felt about Charlie and the ugly gossip.

"Charlie," Jake said—and he wondered how he'd sounded, saying the name.

urious? Well, he was.

nan would be, when a rich guy left a

uple of hundred thousand acres

land, no matter how tumble-

se not...

?"

Addison shut the refrigerator door and turned toward him.

"Charles Hilton."

Her tone was wary, maybe even defiant. So was the look in her eyes.

Okay. Now Jake knew exactly how he'd sounded.

Like a man biting back a mouthful of jealousy.

"He was my friend." She waited. "I told you that, remember?"

"Hey. I didn't say—"

"You didn't have to."

"Addison. Honey. That's not fair. I only meant—"

He frowned. Why was he explaining himself? They'd met, what, two days ago? One day ago? He was losing track. She had her own life, just as he had his.

Hell. Be honest, Wilde.

Plain and simple, he wanted to know if she was carrying the torch for a dead guy.

"I meant," he said slowly, "did you love him?"

"Didn't you hear what I said? He was my friend. My God, you're like all the rest, believing what you want to bel—"

Jake cursed, dragged Addison to her toes and kissed her.

Not gently.

Not tenderly.

His kiss was demanding and possessive, and yet so sweet it took her all of a heartbeat to respond to it. Her lips parted; her tongue slid against his. And when he took the kiss deeper, she put her arms around his neck and gave herself up to the feel of him against her.

"I'm sorry, Adoré," he said. "I believe you. And even if you had loved him—"

"I did love him. Like a father. And he loved me like a daughter."

Jake nodded. "Good," he said thickly. "Because I don't think I could handle his ghost haunting you and this godforsaken ranch."

There was a silence. Then she gave a soft laugh.

"Jacob. That doesn't even make sense."

It made perfect sense to him. Or maybe not. Hadn't he just told himself that he'd only met this woman a day ago? That he had no claim on her?

More to the point, he didn't want a claim on her. On anybody.

Why would he, when he was moving on?

"Jake?"

"Yeah." He expelled a long breath. Stick to the facts, he told himself. Facts were always safe. "So, what kind of guy was he?"

She smiled. "You'd have liked him. He was very down-to-earth."

"Was he your boss?"

"A colleague, but a thousand times the lawyer I'll ever be."

"I'll bet you're Clarence Darrow in a skirt."

She laughed.

"If I'm any good at all, it's Charlie's doing. He was my mentor." She smiled. "I used to call him my hero."

A muscled flickered in Jake's temple.

"There are no such things as heroes," he said, "except in fairy tales."

Addison touched her hand to his face.

"You're a hero," she said softly.

"The hell I am. I did what I was trained to do."

"Sometimes," she said, even more softly, "doing what you're trained to do is what heroism is all about."

Jake snorted. "That's media B.S."

"No, it's the truth." She hesitated. "My father was a fireman."

"Yeah, well, no question. Those guys are heroes."

"He was trained to go into burning buildings. The last time he went into one, he died."

"Hell, Adoré. How old were—"

"Six. And I still remember how I loved him, and how brave he was."

"This isn't the same."

"It is. You saved lives."

His jaw tightened. "You, of all people, should know better than to believe every story you hear."

"Jacob—"

He moved past her, opened the refrigerator door.

"I thought we were going to get something to eat."

Addison couldn't see his face but she had a clear view of his scar, and of the rigidity of his shoulders, as if he'd been cast in stone.

She'd touched a nerve, and she—she cared for him too much to touch it again.

"Right," she said briskly. She stepped in front of him and made a show of checking the shelves she'd checked five minutes before. "Let's see. I have yogurt. Cottage cheese. Wheat bread. Tomatoes and lettuce and, oh, some tofu…"

Nothing. She could feel him standing behind her, something—anger, pain, despair—coming off him like waves of heat.

"Tofu, then," she said brightly. "Mixed with granola. And toasted wheat bread topped with cottage—"

Jake reached past her and shut the door.

"The basic food groups," he said, turning her toward him.

The darkness was gone. His posture had eased. There was even what might have been the beginning of a smile on his lips.

She smiled, too, and offered a silent thank-you to the gods for giving women the instinctive knowledge that the mention of fermented milk and soybeans could drag a man like Jacob back to reality.

"I'm going to buy you dinner." There it was, a real smile, and it made her heart lift. "Or breakfast. Or lunch. Or whatever meal this is supposed to be."

"At midnight? In the middle of nowhere?"

"Get that look off your face, Adoré. Anybody would think you're suggesting Wilde's Crossing can't hold its own with the gourmet dee-lites of the Big Apple."

She snorted. Jake's smile became a grin.

"How about a small wager?"

"Fifty cents. And, just so we have the ground rules straight, McDonald's won't do it."

"Fifty cents,' he scoffed. "You call that a bet?"

Addison cocked her head. "Suggest something."

He put his arms around her, laced his hands together in the small of her back.

"How about if I win, we'll replace that yogurt with whipped cream?"

A rosy pink glazed her cheeks. "Whipped cream and granola?" she said, batting her lashes in feigned innocence. "I don't know."

"Whipped cream and you," Jake answered, his words low and gruff. "Your mouth. Your breasts. Your thighs."

Addison rose on her toes and planted a quick kiss on his lips.

"Deal," she whispered, "just as long as we save some of that whipped cream for me to use on you."

He groaned. She laughed. And before he could push her back against the refrigerator door and show her that they didn't need whipped cream at all, she slipped out of his encircling arms and headed out of the kitchen, her hips swaying with what he knew was deliberate, teasing provocation.

He laughed....

But then his laughter died.

In its place was a sensation he'd never felt before. He wanted to go after her, scoop her into his arms and make love to her, sure.

But he wanted more.

More than taking her to bed.

He wanted her in his heart, in his life....

You? a cold voice inside him said. *Don't be stupid, man.*

"Come on, slowpoke. Get your shirt... Jake?"

He blinked. She was waiting for him just outside the kitchen. She had a sweater over her arm.

"Hey," she said softly. "What's the matter?"

He shook his head. "Nothing."

"You sure? Seriously, I can scramble some eggs if you don't want to—"

He was beside her in a heartbeat; she was in his arms in less than that and when he kissed her, the kiss was so deep, so intense, that she let the sweater fall to the floor so she could cling to him for support.

Something was wrong. She knew it. And she could only hope that he would tell her what it was because whatever it took, she'd help him.

How would a woman not help a man once she realized she was falling in love with him?

It turned out, he couldn't wear his shirt.

"No buttons," he said, and gave her a solemn look. "People see me wearing a shirt without buttons, they'll know you tore them off."

That rated another blush.

Thankfully, old man Chambers had not been one to toss things out. The ancient equipment in some of the outbuildings, the sagging furniture and antique appliances in the house, were testament to his frugality.

The jeans and workshirts Jake had years ago left, in the closet in what the old man had called the hired hand's room, were still there.

The jeans were threadbare but a couple of the shirts were usable. He retrieved a blue one. It was too tight but that was the least of his worries.

The real problem was trying to figure out what was going on with him.

They were on the way to breakfast, and he was driving like a man possessed. The speedometer needle hit ninety and kept on going. He always drove fast but tonight—

Tonight, he wished the car was a small,

sleek jet that could carry them high above the clouds.

He needed to feel the world fall away below him.

What the hell had happened back in that kitchen? One minute they'd been laughing, teasing each other with memories of the long day they'd spent in bed, anticipating the hours still ahead, and then, all of a sudden, sex hadn't been enough.

Enough for what?

Jake shot a glance at Addison.

That, as the Danish prince had said a long time ago, was the question.

There'd been that other moment, too, when the truth of his own life had forced its way into his thoughts. Memories of the night he'd lost those men.

Men?

Jake shifted his weight, flexed his hands on the steering wheel.

Boys. Eighteen. Nineteen. The oldest had been twenty-one. And they'd died because he'd been too late, too late, too late—

"Jacob?"

Addison touched his arm. He damn near jumped out of his skin. It took a minute to remember where he was.

Who he was with.

A woman who knew nothing about him except that he was supposed to be some kind of hero.

"Jacob," she said again, "we're going awfully fast."

He looked at the speedometer. Eased his foot off the gas until they were down to a reasonable speed.

Like ninety.

"Is something wrong?"

"No," he said quickly. "Everything's fine."

He wanted to tell her. He ached for it. The sweet relief that would come of telling her that he didn't deserve the medals, the adulation, the nonsense the world had heaped on him.

He couldn't.

What if she looked at him the way he looked at himself each morning? Looked at him with disappointment and, worse still, disgust?

Angie's was right ahead, the sign—Angie's Café, Open 24 Hours—blinking on and off as it had always done.

Thank God for small favors, he thought, as he pulled into the parking lot and turned off the engine.

"See?" he said brightly. "What'd I tell you? Angie's is never closed. Of course, you won't find tofu on the menu…"

Her silver eyes were filled with question.

He cursed, reached for her, took her in his arms and held her against his heart.

"Stop worrying about me," he said softly. "I'm fine."

She wasn't buying it. He could see it in her face.

"Honey." His voice roughened. "I just need—I need what you've given me, okay? This day. This night." He paused. "Most of all, I need you."

It was the truth.

He wasn't sure what that meant or where it was taking him.

The only certainty was that what was going on inside him scared the hell out of him.

CHAPTER TEN

ANGIE'S CAFÉ was warm and brightly lit.

It was also as busy as any place in Times Square would have been at this hour.

A plump woman looked up when they came in. Her eyes widened and she rushed out from behind the counter, greeted Jake with a squeal and a hug. He lifted her off her feet, spun her around as if she weighed no more than a feather.

"You come home to make an honest woman outta me, Jake Wilde?"

Jake grinned.

"If I ever settle down, Angie, it'll surely be with you."

The woman laughed and Jake made quick introductions. Angie looked at Addison from head to toe, then nodded her approval and led them to one of the red vinyl booths that lined the walls.

Jake waved away the menu.

"Don't need it, Angie. I've been dreaming of one of your breakfasts for months."

Angie grinned.

"Eggs over easy. Bacon. Home fries. Biscuits. Grits. And buckets and buckets of coffee."

Jake smiled. "Add some sausage and you've got it."

"How 'bout you, miss? You want the same?"

Addison looked up from the menu.

"Do you have Egg Beaters?"

Jake snorted. Addison ignored him.

"If not," she said politely, "then I'd like one poached egg on wheat toast. No butter on the toast."

"And?"

"And, that's it. Oh, coffee, please, with a packet of the blue stuff or the pink stuff instead of sugar."

"One regular breakfast," Angie said. "One poached egg, wheat toast and grits."

"No grits, thank you."

"Grits," Angie said, tucking her pencil behind her ear and walking away.

"No. Wait. I don't want—"

"It's got nothing to do with what you want, Adoré," Jake said patiently. "You're south of the Mason-Dixon Line. Grits come with everything."

"Mason and Dixon were surveyors," Addison said, with a toss of her head, "not chefs."

"They were Northerners."

She raised an eyebrow. He'd said it the way someone else might say, *They were barbarians.*

"News flash, Jacob. So am I."

He grinned. "Yeah, and I've decided to look beyond that."

She stuck her tongue out.

"You're trying to distract me," he said in a throaty growl.

She gave him a saccharine-sweet smile. "Is it working?"

"Want to find out?" he said with a deliberate leer as he reached for her hand.

"Behave yourself," she scolded, but her smile turned warm and real.

"I'll behave if you try the grits. Who knows? You might like 'em."

"Trust me, Captain—"

"Lieutenant," Jake said quickly, and suddenly his teasing smile was gone.

"But I thought—"

"Promotions and medals go together."

Was that irony or bitterness in his voice? She couldn't tell.

"I don't understand."

"They give you a medal, they up your rank. Simple as that."

She knew it couldn't possibly be as simple as that. And she saw the darkness in his face again. *Talk to me, Jacob,* she wanted to say…

"I was a lieutenant for a long time. It's what my men called me. It's what I still am, inside. Okay?"

There was no disputing that *okay.* Addison nodded.

"You must be glad to be back."

His fingers wrapped around hers.

"I am. And I'm not." He gave a rueful laugh. "Man, I'm really decisive, aren't I?"

"It can't be easy, coming home after everything you saw."

He looked at her. "What I saw is that the world isn't what I grew up thinking it was."

"It's not the place hardly anyone grows up thinking it is."

He knew she was right, but it went deeper than that for him. When you grew up on tales of heroes and warriors, when men fought and died for reasons that were always clear and always honorable…

"No," he said, after a minute, "it isn't." Jake turned his hand palm-up so that their fingers were intertwined. "Tell me about your father," he said. "Losing him must have been tough for you and your mom."

Her silver eyes darkened.

"It was awful. I adored him. He understood me, you know? I wasn't into dolls or stuff. I loved reading and math and science."

He smiled. "The future lawyer, hard at work."

She smiled, too. "He used to tell me to grow up strong and independent enough to be whatever I wanted."

"Good advice," Jake said softly. "He sounds like a great guy."

"He was." She swallowed hard. "Did I tell you he went back into that burning building because a little boy was trapped?" She nodded, looked down at their joined hands. "The roof collapsed on both of them."

"Honey. I'm sorry. I shouldn't have—"

"The boy's mother came to see us. She wanted us to know what my father's heroism had meant to her."

A muscle bunched in his jaw.

"Even though she'd lost her child."

"Yes. Like those policemen and firemen who lost their lives on 9/11. They died heroes."

She was right. Of course they had. Heroes did the right thing. It was the determination to do that right thing that mattered.

But if a man wanted to do the right thing and didn't do it, nothing else he'd done could possibly make him a hero.

"Everything was different after that. My mother—my mother couldn't deal with his loss. Things went downhill. We lost our house and she—she changed." She gave him a small, obviously painful smile. "He was a hero but I wish he'd come home to us, you know?"

He knew.

He knew, absolutely.

Heroism was in the eye of the beholder.

Coming home…

Coming home was everything. He'd known that from the beginning—but what if you couldn't bring all your men home…?

"Breakfast," Angie announced, and slapped two huge platters of food on the table in front of them.

Addison looked at hers. Two eggs, over easy. Bacon. Sausages. Biscuits.

Grits.

"Fry cook said he don't know how to poach eggs," Angie said cheerfully. "And turns out we're all out of wheat bread." She put her hands on her ample hips. "But I left off the home fries. Figured you was one of them health-food nuts, or somethin'."

"Or something," Addison said, still staring at the food.

"You try those grits, girl. They'll put meat on your bones. Texas men like their ladies with somethin' they can grab hold of. Right, Jake?"

Jake tried not to laugh.

"Absolutely," he said.

Addison narrowed her eyes at him as Angie walked away.

He was the very picture of innocence.

And he was waiting.

Okay.

What were a couple of pounds compared to the challenge in her lover's eyes?

She looked at the grits, picked up her fork and dug it into the cooked, coarsely ground corn.

"I'll get you for this, Jacob Wilde," she said, trying to sound stern as she brought the fork to her mouth.

Jake waggled his eyebrows. "God, I hope so."

She glared at him. Then her lips curved and she burst into laughter.

"Me, too," she said—and that was the moment when Jake realized that against all odds, despite the ugly reality of his life, his smart, sexy, sophisticated-but-trailer-park-tough Adoré was starting to mean something to him.

Something that scared the hell out of him even to contemplate.

They drove home with the windows down and the radio on, singing along with Willie and then Waylon.

Well, no, Addison thought, as Jake switched stations so he could harmonize with Johnny Cash. He was singing. She only hummed.

She'd never listened to country music before tonight.

Turned out, she liked it.

The lyrics were honest and real.

Like her Jacob.

He was a man who'd grown up with wealth, and yet there was no pretension to him. He was a warrior, and yet he could be tender.

But there was a darkness in him that had to do with the war.

Travis and Caleb hadn't told her much, only that he wasn't comfortable in the role of hero.

She could understand modesty, especially now that she knew him, but there was more to it than that….

"Addison?"

She swung toward her lover.

She'd been so deep in thought that she hadn't even realized they'd reached the ranch and were parked in the driveway.

Her heart swelled at the way he was looking at her.

"My Adoré," he said softly, and she stopped thinking and went into his waiting arms.

The first faint light of dawn, touching the bedroom with crimson and gold streamers, woke him.

Addison was curled against him, sound asleep.

Jake looked at her, drinking in her beauty, her honesty, her essence.

He had never known a woman like her.

No pretense. No girlish gushing. No treating him with breathless wonder because he was rich or because he was a so-called hero. No averting her eyes from his damaged face or displays of cloying sympathy,

He just made her happy.

God knew, she did the same for him.

He was happy. And he'd never expected to feel that way again.

Gently, he kissed her bare shoulder.

Then he rose from the bed as carefully as possible, so he wouldn't wake her.

He pulled on his jeans, made a face when he realized that though they'd showered a couple of times, he hadn't changed them in—hell, in however many days he'd been here.

He'd lost track of time.

Was it Sunday? Monday? It was important to know. Addison had told him she was leaving at the end of the week.

He didn't want to think about that now.

He'd also lost track of the fact that his family might be wondering what had happened to him.

He stepped out on the porch, took his cell phone from his pocket and hit the speed-dial button for *El Sueño.* It was early, but he was counting on the fact that Lissa had always been an early riser.

She answered on the second ring.

"Hi," he said, "it's me. Just figured I'd let you guys know I'm still alive."

"We came to that conclusion on our own,

otherwise, we'd have had a call from the hospital or the police."

"Liss. I'm sorry—"

"It's okay. You're a big boy, Jake. We didn't expect you to check in."

He rubbed his cheek. The scar under his eye was throbbing. It had a nasty habit of doing that when he did something stupid.

"You're also an idiot."

"Yeah. You'd be amazed how many people have told me that lately."

She laughed. "Wanna bet?" Her tone softened. "You okay?"

"I'm fine."

"But not fine enough to put down roots here, where you belong."

So much for a softening of tone.

"Travis around? Or Caleb?"

Her sigh echoed through the phone.

"Trav drove to Dallas. Caleb had an appointment in Austin. Em and Jaimie are gone, too. They both flew back to New York. And I'm out of here in about half an hour."

Jake ran a hand through his hair.

"Nobody waited for me? I mean—"

"I know what you mean. The thing is, we've been waiting almost two years. We love you like crazy but—"

"Yeah. I get it."

"Do you?"

Silence. Then Lissa cleared her throat. "The General called. He said he wished he could have gotten home to see you."

"I've heard the speech before."

"Haven't we all?" His sister sighed. "If I didn't know better, I'd say he really meant it this time."

"Yes," Jake said flatly. "But you do know better. So do I."

"So, what's next? You're still leaving town?"

Jake hesitated. He thought of Addison, asleep in the bedroom….

"Jake?"

"I—I'm not sure what my plans are right now."

"Well, keep in touch, okay? And, Jake… even though we both know you're a jerk, of all my brothers, I love you the most."

He knew she'd meant to make him laugh, and he obliged.

"You know, kid, we figured out that routine years ago. It's what you tell each of us."

"Yes." She laughed, too. "But at the moment I say it, I mean it." She hesitated. "Come visit me in California, okay?"

"My sister, the chef to the stars."

Lissa blew a raspberry into the phone. "Your sister, the dork who gets to clean up the mess made by the chef to the stars."

They both laughed, she made kissy sounds, Jake said he loved her and put his phone in his pocket.

He hadn't asked Lissa what was going to happen to *El Sueño.*

If he didn't run it, who would? Ranching was never simple but running The Dream was the equivalent of running a privately held, exceedingly successful corporation.

Horses. Crops. Mineral rights. Oil. And a seemingly endless list of businesses in which the ranch was invested.

The Dream had always been well-managed but there'd been a time Jake had been filled with ideas on how to do even bigger and better things with it.

Taking over as CEO would be his chance.

It would also be a reason to stay on in Wilde's Crossing, take the time to see where this thing, whatever it was, with Addison was going.

Which was nuts.

It wasn't going anywhere.

How could it?

There was no place in his life for her. Even he knew his head was totally screwed up.

Yeah, but maybe it wasn't quite as screwed up anymore.

After all, here he was, thinking about staying. No guarantees, but—

But what?

What would he say to her?

Jake got to his feet.

Stay here. Don't go back to New York. I don't know what I'm offering you, I don't know what tomorrow will bring, I only know I don't want you to leave me....

Right.

That certainly summed it up.

He didn't know this, he didn't know that. The truth was, he didn't know anything. He didn't even know himself anymore, and neither did she.

Nobody did.

He hadn't had the nightmare since he and Addison had been together, but what did that mean?

The dream would come back.

It always did.

The Blackhawk. The pass through the mountains. The flames. The explosion. The smoke and the screams and the sight of men being blown apart, and all because he hadn't been where he knew, goddammit, he *knew* he should have been…

A pair of arms wrapped around him from the rear.

Jake spun around, hands fisted, lips drawn back in a snarl…and saw Addison, her face gone white.

"I'm sorry, Jacob. I didn't mean to startle you…."

"No. I'm the one who's sorry. I don't know why—"

But he did. He knew why, that the nightmares, the trigger-sharp reactions, the need to keep moving before everything caught up and took him by the throat…

All of it had become part of him.

Walk away now, Jake told himself. His Adoré deserved a man who was whole.

Instead, he held out his arms. She went into them. He drew her close and buried his face in her hair. And when she lifted her face to his, he bent to her and kissed her and kissed her until nothing mattered but them.

The morning's darkness faded away.

They drove into town.

At first, Addison was uneasy.

People recognized Jake's Thunderbird.

They stared. And stood stock-still, taking it all in when Jake parked in the supermarket lot, took Addison in his arms and waltzed her to the door as music poured from the store's loudspeaker.

"Jacob," she blurted, "people will talk!"

"Let 'em," he replied, and he dipped her back over his arm when they reached the door, brought her upright and dropped a kiss on the tip of her nose.

Somebody cheered.

Addison blushed.

And then, without warning, she thought, *He's right. Let them talk. Let everybody talk. I don't care.*

Amazing.

That she didn't care.

She always had, before.

A girl whose mother tipped over the edge of reason with breathtaking swiftness, who went from being a grieving widow to being the town joke in the pink trailer down by the railroad tracks, was a girl who grew up wanting to avoid being looked at by anybody and everybody.

She'd only gone home once after she left

for college, and that had been to attend her mother's funeral.

Nobody had recognized her. Or talked about her. Why would they? She'd learned to blend in.

Anonymity was her armor, until Charlie.

But she'd endured the talk and pointed fingers because she'd loved him.

Charlie, who'd been her friend.

Now, they would talk about her because of Jacob.

Jacob, who was her lover…

A tremor swept through her.

"What is it, honey?"

"Nothing," she said, and she busied herself choosing a head of leaf lettuce as if the future of the world depended on it, because she couldn't trust herself to say another word.

After all, what could you say when you'd just faced facts?

Jacob wasn't only her lover.

He was her love.

They bought steaks and salad stuff, bread and cheese and wine. Then they drove a block to the Western Ware Shop, where Jake bought jeans and shirts so he'd have a change of clothes.

And though Addison protested, he bought her boots.

"There's a law in Texas," he told her solemnly. "It says, if you own a ranch, you have to own boots."

The owner, who turned out to be the buxom blonde with the Dolly Parton hair and a nice person after all, chuckled and agreed.

By the time they headed back to the ranch, it was midafternoon. Just enough time, Jake said, to take a serious look around the place.

Unless she wanted him to saddle horses and take a ride—if she knew how to ride.

"Certainly, I can ride," she told him.

Not really.

They went out to the paddock, where the kid who worked the ranch part-time had left the few horses the old man had owned.

Jake watched Addison eye the animals from all angles.

"You sure you can ride?" he said, not even trying to mask his skepticism.

"Didn't I tell you I could?"

"When's the last time you were on a horse?"

She sucked her bottom lip between her teeth. The sight almost made him forget all about horses.

"It's been a while."

Jake folded his arms. "Adoré. Answer the question."

She shrugged. "A couple of years."

"How many is a couple?"

She lifted her head, eyed him with defiance.

"There was a fair in town one summer. And there were pony rides…."

Okay. She couldn't ride. Jake smiled and promised to teach her one day.

She smiled, too. It was his first mention of a shared future.

Old man Chambers had owned a decrepit truck. Jake filled it with gasoline, fiddled with the engine, started it up.

They spent a couple of hours, driving and looking around.

Addison glowed.

She loved the view of the distant blue hills. The antelopes that watched them, ears and tails twitching. The blush of early spring wildflowers. The creek that tumbled over a pile of copper-colored rocks.

Jake took mental note of all that needed doing. Fences required repair. Roads needed grading. Acreage where crops should have been growing needed tilling.

But if he shut his eyes, he could see what could be done here.

The land had all kinds of promise.

If a man knew what he was doing…

A man like him…

It was a foolish thought. He wasn't staying in Wilde's Crossing. It just—hell, it just felt so right, being here, being with his Adoré….

Jake stopped the old truck, made a U-turn and headed for the house.

"We're going back so soon?" Addison said.

He nodded.

"I need you," he said simply, and her heart seemed to dance because she needed him, too.

Forever.

They made love.

And showered.

Addison dried her hair. When she came back to the bedroom, Jake was dressed in his new jeans and one of his new shirts.

"Ta da," he said, turning toward her….

He'd left off his eye patch.

He had not been without it, even once. Not in bed or in the shower or while she slept in his arms.

It was so much a part of him that she'd forgotten it existed.

Evidently, so had he—until that moment, when he caught a glimpse of himself in the dresser mirror.

"Crap," he said, and he clapped his hand over the empty socket.

Addison flew across the room, grabbed his wrist with a strength that shocked him.

"Don't…you…dare," she said through her teeth. "Do you hear me, Jacob? Don't you dare apologize or cover your eye or do anything other than look at me and listen when I say it doesn't matter. Your eye. Your wounds." She dragged his hand from his face, kissed it, then held it tightly in both of hers. "Nothing matters but you. That you lived. That you came home. That I—that I—"

She was weeping. It took Jake a little while to realize that he was weeping, too.

CHAPTER ELEVEN

ADDISON MADE coffee, and they took it out to the enclosed back porch.

She sat in an old wicker chair. He stretched out on an equally old wicker sofa. They talked about the ranch, the sunset, and then Jake cleared his throat.

"Adoré." A muscle knotted in his jaw. "I need to talk to you."

Her heart skipped a beat.

"You can talk to me about anything, Jacob," she said quietly.

He sat up and held out his hand.

"Come and sit with me."

She went to him and he tugged her down next to him.

"We have to get things straight," he said, after a minute. "The hero thing, I mean." His voice was low. "See, I'm not any kind of hero."

What he'd said might have been modesty or humility, but Addison knew it was more. She bit her lip, determined to keep quiet until he'd finished.

"I told you that I flew Blackhawks."

She nodded. She could feel the tension radiating through him.

"Blackhawks are big. Tough. They can handle mostly anything you ask of them. My men were the same. They were a remarkable bunch of guys."

Were. He kept saying *were.*

"Our work was dangerous. Not all the time. Sometimes, it was boring as hell. Anybody in that kind of life—cops, soldiers, firemen like your dad—can tell you that. One minute, you're up to your ass in adrenaline and the next, you're struggling to keep awake."

"There must have been times that were terrifying."

"There were. Only a fool isn't afraid, Adoré, but you don't really think about fear. You think about your mission. Getting in and getting out. Philosophizing about war is for historians. Talking about it is for politicians. Surviving it is for soldiers, and that means you and the guy beside you fighting to keep each other alive."

Addison waited. At last, she put her hand on Jake's thigh.

"But something went wrong," she said softly.

He nodded. Put down his glass. Rose to his feet. Walked to the windows, stared blindly at the scarlet sun.

"A squad went out on fairly routine patrol. They were heading back when some old man waved them down, told them a high-level al Qaeda operative had taken refuge in a village maybe six, seven klicks away."

Jake jammed his hands into his pockets.

"They called in the info. Problem was, waiting for backup could mean losing the target."

"So they went in themselves."

Jake nodded again. "Straight into an ambush." His voice was so low she had to strain to hear it. "In a narrow mountain pass. They were being cut to shreds."

Addison got to her feet. "Jake," she said, "you don't have to—"

"I do," he said gruffly. "You need to know. Or maybe I need to tell you. Either way, it's time I talked about it."

She stood next to him, wanting to put her

arms around him, settling for laying her hand on his arm.

"We went in after them." He flashed a bitter smile. "It's called an extraction. I guess that sounds better than the reality, which is that you're going after men who are often already dead or dying."

"You rescued them."

"We got the wounded. And the lucky ones who hadn't been hit. We got the dead, too. We got them all…at least, we thought we did."

He rubbed his hand and over the back of his head.

"Except, we found out we'd left two men behind." He turned toward her, his face gray. "You don't leave men behind, Addison. Not even the dead—and certainly not ones who are still alive. So it was a no-brainer. We had to go back. I knew it. My crew knew it. We were all agreed."

"Couldn't another Blackhawk have gone in?"

"There was no other Blackhawk. We were it." His voice became a low growl. "We needed to go back. But the son-of-a-bitch colonel in charge wouldn't give the order."

The dying sun had painted stripes of scarlet

over Jake's cheeks, turning him into a warrior from an earlier time.

"He must have had his reasons," Addison said. "Maybe—maybe he didn't want to risk more lives…."

"He didn't give a flying fig about lives. He was a congressman's son." Jake slammed his fist against the window frame; it shuddered beneath the blow. "Some kind of mix-up a couple of days before had dumped him on us instead of putting him behind the desk that was waiting for him."

"So he had no experience."

"He had no balls. His old man was one of the loudest voices demanding what he called fiscal responsibility. And Blackhawks cost a fortune, maybe six, seven million bucks. This bastard was scared stiff of Daddy. So he sat on his political ass and played with himself while time began running out."

The first time Addison had heard about Jake, that he was some kind of hero, she wouldn't have been able to figure out how the story ended.

Now, she'd shared his thoughts, his life, his bed.

She knew what came next.

"You went back anyway," she said.

"I argued with him. I screamed at him. Finally, I got him alone and swore I'd kill him if he didn't give the order." He flashed a cold smile. "And he knew I'd do it."

"So he gave the order."

"Yes. But we'd lost too much precious time. They'd already—already dealt with the men we'd hoped to save. They were dead—we could see their mutilated bodies as I brought us in. And they'd brought in heavier weapons."

"Oh, God, Jacob..."

"They blew us apart. Killed my crew. And I—I killed them. Every last mothering one..."

His voice broke. Addison stepped in front of him.

"How can you blame yourself? It wasn't your fault. You did everything you could. You did more."

"I should have ignored my orders," he said bitterly.

"But you did ignore them. You forced your commanding officer to take action."

"Too late. All of it was too late. They gave me a promotion I didn't want and a medal I didn't deserve."

"And him? The colonel??"

Jake gave a bitter laugh.

"He got a medal, too. And a promotion. To the Pentagon. Now his face is all over the media, and when they tell him what a hero he is, he looks modest and makes sure the camera gets him at his best angle."

Addison took her lover's hands in hers.

"My father would have been proud to shake your hand," she said softly. "He'd have been as proud to know you as I am."

Jake made a strangled sound. Then he reached for her and wrapped her in his arms.

How had he gotten so lucky?

How had this miracle happened?

A handful of days ago, he'd been a hollow man existing in a bleak world, tormented by memories that were destroying him.

Addison had changed everything.

He woke with her in his arms, fell asleep the same way. And he slept through the night.

The dreams were gone.

No more flames, clawing the sky.

No more twisted metal, shrieking like a wounded beast as the Blackhawk was torn apart.

No more men bleeding into the thin mountain soil.

For almost two years, everybody—the

doctors, the therapists, the nurses, his family, every last one of them—had told him he needed to deal with what was inside him.

The wounds that he kept hidden.

See a shrink, they said. Join a support group. Talk it out.

And now, he had.

He'd emptied his soul, let Addison, his Adoré, see the ugliness that had been killing him.

And after she'd heard it all, she'd said she was proud to know him….

God, how he loved her.

Loved her with all his heart.

He hadn't told her that. Not yet. He was afraid to because this involved so much.

It meant saying, *I love you, I want to spend my life with you, and can you give up your entire existence for me?*

What if she said no?

What if she liked him but she didn't love him?

He couldn't bear to think about the possibility.

He needed to get out of here. Get her out of here. Take her someplace romantic…

Romantic, he thought, and he realized he knew the perfect place.

* * *

He told her they were going out for supper.

"Out?"

"Out," he said kissing the tip of her nose. "Put on something fancy. That black dress you wore the first time we met. Those shoes."

She batted her lashes at him.

"You like those shoes, huh?"

Jake grinned. "Enough so I went back and found the one you lost."

"Okay. Black silk dress. Stiletto heels. Give me half an hour."

"Twenty minutes," he said, and he turned her toward the stairs, gave her a gentle swat on the backside and told his heart to slow down or he'd never make it through the night.

She was halfway up the stairs when he called after her.

"Addison?"

She turned and looked at him.

"So you're not, you know, homesick for New York?"

Addison swept the tip of her tongue over suddenly dry lips.

"No. I'm not homesick at all. I—I like it here, Jacob. Much, much more than I'd thought I would."

He stared at her. She stared at him.

Tell me you love me and you want me to stay, she thought.

Tell her you love her and you want her to stay, he thought.

"You'll like Dallas, too," he said.

"What?"

"That's where we're going for dinner."

"Dallas is a two-hour drive!"

He grinned. "Not when I'm behind the wheel, remember?"

She wore the black dress. The black heels.

He thought about stripping the dress off her so that she was wearing just the heels and the thong and matching scrap of a bra he figured she'd be wearing underneath.

Then he told himself to behave.

He was taking her to a restaurant he hadn't been to in years, and he could have her all to himself when they got home.

He wore his new jeans, a new black T-shirt with a leather jacket over it—she'd admired it at the store that morning and he'd bought it, more for her than for him. He even polished his boots for the occasion.

And he had on his black eye patch.

Under it, in the socket where his eye had

once been, he wore a silicone thing called a conformer.

Eventually, he'd have an artificial eye made to put in its place.

He'd been putting that off, or maybe not putting it off so much as not being ready to deal with looking in the mirror and seeing something designed to make him look more like the man he'd once been when he wasn't that man…

Hell.

Why tiptoe through that mental morass? The simple fact was, it was time to get the eye made, and he would do it.

He drove fast, but the time would have raced by even if he hadn't because they talked all the way to the city.

There was so much to learn about each other. So many things they had in common, even if with a slight twist.

He loved football. The Dallas Cowboys.

"Such a surprise," she said with wide-eyed innocence, and laughed when he tossed the words back at her a minute later, after she said she loved football, too, but for her, it was the New York Jets.

"Such a surprise," he said. "Well, nobody is perfect."

They both loved dogs. Wood fires on cold winter evenings, good California red wine, crusty French bread and the beach very early in the morning.

By the time they reached the restaurant Jake had chosen for this, their very first real date, he was struggling not to turn to her and say, *I love one more thing, Adoré. I love you.*

That would wait until later.

The maître d'hotel led them to a table with a view of a delicately lit garden.

Addison was entranced.

"Oh, it's perfect!" she said softly.

Wrong, Jake knew.

Addison was what perfection was all about.

The question was, did she love him? Every sigh, every smile, every touch of her hand told him that she did.

Still, it was hard to put his heart on the line.

And a lot to ask of a woman, to give up the life she knew for one she didn't.

Could she trade New York for Wilde's Crossing?

Could he trade it for New York, if it came down to that?

He knew this was where he belonged. Not

just in Texas, not just in Wilde's Crossing, but on *El Sueño,* where the very land held the blood and bones of his forebears, those who'd fought, sweated and died for the privilege to call the land theirs.

A few days ago, all he'd wanted was to get away from this place.

He'd been a man on the run. From the past, from an uncertain future.

From himself.

He'd had to keep moving. Like a shark, staying in one place would have drowned him.

Not anymore.

He was in control of his life again. He was certain of it. From this point on, he could only move forward.

His heart swelled as he looked at Addison. He'd brought her to the right place. Small. Intimate. Elegant, complete with a small dance floor.

Jake pushed back his chair and got to his feet.

"Miss McDowell. Will you dance with me?"

Her smile lit the room.

"I'd be honored."

He took her in his arms and knew, without question, that was where she would always belong.

Dinner was wonderful.

Addison knew New York wasn't the only city in the world but she was a born and bred New Yorker.

Nothing could match her town.

It turned out that Dallas could.

The restaurant was spectacular. The food was glorious. Wild mushroom bisque. Broiled sea scallops with braised radicchio. Champagne.

And Jacob. Mostly, Jacob.

Her Jacob.

He was gorgeous. There wasn't a woman in the room who hadn't looked at him with lust in her eyes.

And he was attentive. Funny. Charming. She loved dancing with him. He held her close; she could feel every inch of his long, wonderful body against hers.

She could smell his scent, sexy and natural and male as she burrowed into him.

And—and *what are you doing, Addison McDowell?*

Well, she knew what she was doing.

She was thinking about all that and she was turning herself on....

"Addison."

She swallowed hard. Leaned back in Jake's arms and looked up at him.

"Yes?"

He laughed. It was a soft, very sexy sound.

"I know what you're thinking, Adoré," he said.

She laughed, too.

"What are you going to do about it?" she said.

They were in the Thunderbird and roaring along the highway not more than three or four minutes later.

Jake had dumped a handful of bills on their table and all but carried her from the restaurant.

His mind was a blur.

He hadn't told her he loved her, but he would—just as soon as he could form a coherent sentence.

Right now, he needed to make love to her.

And, hell, even the way he drove, it would be more than an hour before they were alone.

He thought about going to a hotel but humble as it was, okay, ramshackle as it was, the

Chambers place—her place—had become their home.

Except…

Except, God, he was burning up with hunger.

It was the same for her.

She was sitting as close to him as possible, her hand on his thigh. She was trembling, and when he put his hand in her lap, slid it under her skirt, she made a sound that almost drove him insane.

"Jacob," she whispered, "don't. You can't—"

He could.

She gave a breathless little cry as he pushed his fingers past the bit of lace between her thighs.

She was beyond hot. Beyond wet. He put a finger inside her, felt those honeyed walls close around him.

She cried out.

He groaned.

She turned her face toward him. Bit his shoulder.

The car bucked as he yanked the wheel hard and pulled onto the shoulder.

It was late. The night was inky black. They were alone on the road.

"Let me," he said thickly, "Adoré, let me…."

He stripped away the lace.

She unzipped his fly.

He lifted her and then she was taking him inside her, deep, deep, deep.

She rode him, sobbing his name; he threaded his hands into her hair, brought her face to his so he could kiss her mouth, swallow her cries….

And still, when they were finally at the ranch, they came together as soon as the front door closed behind them, tearing away the clothes that separated them, desperate for each other.

At last, they made their way upstairs, to the bed that had become theirs.

Jake's last thought was of the woman in his arms, and of what he would tell her in the morning.

That he loved her, that he wasn't moving on…

And that he wanted her with him, forever.

The world was on fire.

There were flames everywhere.

Men were screaming. Dying. The Blackhawk was dying, too. It was a beast in pain.

He? He was alive, but drenched in blood.

So much blood. Not only his. The blood of others. Of others…

"Jacob."

He was trapped. Caught in a snake's nest of wires and cables. He tore free of them, began crawling.

"Jake."

Someone was shouting his name. One of his men. Where? Where was he? He couldn't find him. Couldn't see him for the flames, the smoke, the blood that blinded him but he could hear him, screaming in agony, begging for help, for mercy, for Jake to save him…

A hand landed on his shoulder. Tried to pull him back. No. He had to find his men. Had to find—

"Nooo," Jake screamed, and struck out….

"Jacob! Please. Wake up. Wake up! Jake—"

He came awake on a frenzied rush of breath and terror. His heart felt as if it were going to tear free of his chest. His body was soaked with sweat.

At first, he didn't know where he was.

Then he remembered.

The Chambers house. Addison's house now. Her bedroom, gray in the soft wash of early morning light.

He was on the floor, the top sheet and comforter twisted around his legs. The night-table lamp lay smashed beside him.

"Addison," he said hoarsely. "Addison? Dear God, Addison—"

"I'm here, Jacob."

He fought free of the bed linens. She was crouched behind him, face white, eyes enormous. He reached for her, gathered her into his arms.

"Did I hurt you, honey? Did I—"

"No. No, I'm fine."

She wasn't. She was shaking. Her teeth were chattering. He grabbed the comforter, wrapped it around her. "Sweetheart. I'm so sorry…."

Jake drew her tightly against him. That this should have happened, that she should have seen him like this…

"You sure I didn't hurt you? Did I—did I hit you? I know I hit something…"

"The lamp. Not me."

Thank God, he thought, and held her another few seconds. Then he held her from him and looked into her face.

His heart turned over.

Her eyes were wide with shock. Her lips were trembling. She looked as if she had seen all the demons of hell, and she had.

She had seen his demons, and look what they had done to her!

He drew her close again, rocked her in his arms.

"Forgive me, baby."

"There's nothing to forgive. You had a dream, that's all. Just a dream."

Jake felt his muscles tighten.

"It's not *just* a dream, it's *the* dream. I have it over and over, night after goddammed night."

"You haven't had it since we've been together."

She was right. He hadn't. And based on that one fact, he'd tried to tell himself he was okay.

Well, he wasn't okay. He was the same cowardly mess he'd been for almost two years. The only difference was that a dream was no longer simply a dream when it put someone else in danger.

And if that person was a woman you loved…

"I'll make some coffee. Or tea."

She was talking fast; he knew she was upset, although that probably wasn't half the word to describe it. He wanted to hold her closer, tell her how much he loved her….

And because he wanted that more than anything, he let go of her and got to his feet.

Quickly, because he didn't want too much time to think, he grabbed for his clothes and put them on. Shorts. Socks. Jeans.

"Jacob?"

When he yanked his shirt over his head, she took a cotton robe from the back of a chair and pulled it on.

"What are you doing?" she said as he stuffed his feet into his boots. "Please. Listen to me. If you don't want coffee, we could go back to bed for a while and then—"

He swung toward her. The look on his face made her catch her breath.

"Coffee's not going to do it. Neither will sex."

She winced as if he'd hit her. He knew it was a cruel thing to say, a vicious thing to say, but everything inside him was coming apart.

"I know that," she whispered. "I only meant… I care for you, Jacob. You mean—you mean everything to me."

"Wrong," he said sharply. "I don't mean anything to anyone, especially to myself."

"No! You don't mean that."

"Go home, Addison. Go back to New York and your law practice and your life."

"Jacob." Tears blurred her eyes as she hurried through the door after him. "I don't want to leave you. *You* don't want me to leave you. I know you don't."

She was right. He didn't. His life was a mess and so was his head, but he loved her, he would always love her.

That was the very reason he had to leave her.

She deserved a man who was whole. Not a sick, useless coward like him.

He went down the stairs quickly, heard the soft patter of her bare feet behind him. Halfway to the door, he felt the touch of her hand on his shoulder.

Jake hardened his heart and swung toward her.

"The thing is," he said, hating himself for the lie, for the pain he saw shining like tears in her eyes, "this had run its course anyway."

"I don't believe you!"

"You're leaving in a couple of days. I was going to hit the road then, too—I mean, I figured we'd go on having a good time until then—"

"A good time?" she said in a whisper that made him want to tell her he was lying.

He couldn't let that happen.

"I'm sorry if you figured on more from me but you always knew this was a temporary thing. You knew I was moving on."

"Jacob." She sobbed his name, reached her hand toward him. "Jacob, please listen! You need help!"

Jake turned on his heel and walked out.

What he needed, he thought as he got into the Thunderbird, was the open road.

Nobody to question him.

Nobody to make him think or remember when, dammit, all he wanted to do was to forget.

CHAPTER TWELVE

CALEB WILDE sat in his Dallas office, staring out the window.

Any man would do that instead of tending to the letters and files stacked on his desk.

After all, it was one terrific view. The city, its gleaming skyscrapers. Who could keep his mind on work if he had a view like that to distract him?

"Dammit," Caleb muttered, and swung his leather swivel chair back toward his desk.

Lying to himself was pathetic.

He wasn't only ignoring his work, he was ignoring everything, and it didn't have a thing to do with the view.

It had to do with his brother.

Jacob.

Where was he?

Three months had gone by with no word.

Not a note, a phone call, not even an email or a text message.

Well, yeah.

There'd been that one text message, sent to all their phones, his and Travis's, Em's and Lissa's and Jaimie's.

Do not worry about me. I am fine.

Caleb snorted.

What the hell did that mean? That ridiculous phrase, *I am fine.*

Jake was fine.

Really?

"Really?" Caleb said grimly.

How fine could a man be when he'd returned to his home as surly as a hound with a burr up its butt, taken up with a woman he'd wanted no part of, ended up not leaving her side for days and days until, just like that, he vanished.

Jake was gone.

So was Addison.

But they weren't together.

She was back in New York.

He was Christ knew where.

And she wouldn't so much as speak his name.

"I don't know where he is," she'd said when

Caleb phoned her. She'd told Travis the same thing.

And, when they compared notes, they agreed that each time, she'd been choking back tears. Which hadn't kept her from firing the two of them.

"I just don't think it's a good idea to go on working together," was what she'd said.

They couldn't get anything else out of her.

Not that they really wanted to know what had gone wrong between their brother and their client. Their former client.

They'd just hoped she could tell them where Jake was.

Nobody knew.

Aside from that one totally unilluminating text message, he hadn't contacted any of—

The intercom buzzed. Dammit, he wasn't in the mood for interruptions. Hadn't he told that to his PA?

"What?" he barked when he slapped it to life. "I told you, I don't want to be disturbed."

"Yes. I know. But—"

"No 'buts,' Jean. No calls, no messages, no—"

The door opened. Caleb glared at it. Then he shot to his feet.

"Father?"

The General, resplendent in his dress uniform, his chest bristling with ribbons and medals, nodded. "Hello, Caleb."

"You should have... I didn't expect..." Hell, he was running off at the mouth. "Come in, please. If I'd known—"

"There was no time. I flew into D.C. yesterday to meet with— Well, that's unimportant." His father shut the door, strode across the big room to one of the pair of chairs across from the desk and sat. "Please," he said, gesturing, "take a seat."

Caleb nodded. His father was inviting him to sit down in his own chair in his own office.

And he was doing it.

Some other time, he might have laughed. Not today. What was his father doing here? He was not given to dropping in for family visits.

"I am concerned about your brother."

"Travis?"

"Jacob. I am very concerned about him."

What did his father know? Caleb cleared his throat. "Yes. Well, you see—"

The door to his office swung open. Travis stepped into the room, raised his eyebrows and mouthed the words, *What in hell's going on?*

Damned if I know, Caleb wanted to say....

"I hope you don't mind, Caleb. I asked Travis to join us."

"No. That's fi—"

"Take a seat, please, Travis."

Travis nodded. Sat in the chair beside his father. Caleb looked at him. Amazing. The General had taken charge.

"I was just telling your brother that I am concerned about Jacob."

Travis and Caleb looked at each other. They could pretty much read each other's thoughts. They could say, *Why are you concerned?* They could say, *There's nothing to be concerned about.* Or they could be honest, even with this man who had not bothered to return to *El Sueño* for his wounded son's homecoming.

Honesty won out.

"So are we," Caleb said. "We don't know where he is."

"Actually," Travis said, "we do."

Caleb and the General both looked at him.

"We do?"

"He's in Wilde's Crossing. To be specific, he's at the Chambers ranch. The Hilton ranch."

"The McDowell ranch."

Travis shook his head. "It's the Wilde ranch

now. Jake bought it for two million five. That's the only reason I know about it. He wrote a check on his account with my firm and now he owns the place, lock, stock and downed fence posts."

Caleb frowned.

"That doesn't make sense. He turned down the General's offer—your offer, sir—to take over at *El Sueño.* He left Wilde's Crossing. For all we know, he left Texas. Why would he buy the Chambers place?"

"The Wilde place. That's how he refers to it. And I have no idea. He won't answer the phone."

Caleb shot to his feet. "Hell!"

"Exactly."

"You don't think he'd do something stupid—"

"I think he's done a lot of stupid things," Travis said. He stood up. "Like denying that he's one hell of a brave dude. Like refusing to let any of us help him."

"Like walk away from a woman who cared for him."

"Assuming she did."

"People saw them together. They say what they saw was a woman who was crazy about a guy and a guy who was crazy about her."

"Are you two finished with this discussion?"

Surprised, the brothers turned toward the General. Had anyone asked, they'd have said it was impossible to forget he was in the room….

But they just had.

The brothers made eye contact with each other and mentally agreed things had gone crazy.

"Because we don't have time for speculation." Their father rose to his feet. "We must get to the airport as quickly as possible."

Travis narrowed his eyes. "Because, of course," he said coolly, "you have a plane to catch?"

"Because," the General said, "we're flying to Wilde's Crossing."

Jake heard the truck coming minutes before he saw it.

Sounds carried pretty clearly on a still day, especially the sound of a truck. Or an SUV. Something good-sized and fast-moving.

People in a hurry to see him, he thought with a tight smile, and he was sure he knew who they were.

He'd been expecting his brothers to show

up for a couple of days, ever since he'd taken ownership of the ranch.

The noise grew louder, and now he could see a plume of dust rising against the pale blue sky.

The cavalry, riding to the rescue.

He sighed, sat back on his heels, grabbed his discarded T-shirt and mopped his face with it. He looked the shirt over. It was stained, holey, it bore yellow smudges of pollen….

"The hell with it," he said, and pulled it on.

He'd been working outside most of the day, first dealing with the barn, then with the sagging porch steps.

He was tired, his muscles ached, he needed a hot shower and a cold beer.

In other words, he felt fine.

The guys in his group had said physical labor was excellent for giving you enough mental space to help get your head straight.

Turned out they were right.

"Pare your life down to basics," one guy who'd survived Kandahar had told him.

That, too, had been good advice.

Hard work during the day. Meetings a couple of evenings a week. Nights sitting here, on the porch, listening to the crickets and the coyotes. Then bedtime.

Jake had started as a cynic.

Now, he was close to a convert.

The regimen, especially the meetings, the open talk, had made big changes.

Correction.

He'd made big changes. In himself. It was important to know that.

He was in charge of his own life again. It was one hell of a feeling. He still had issues to get through but he could work through them.

The proof was that he slept dreamlessly through the night.

Okay.

Not necessarily dreamlessly. But when he dreamed, it wasn't about fire and screams and death.

He dreamed of Addison. Of what he had lost and would never find again.

No point thinking of that now. The truck—a white SUV—was visible now, and barreling toward him.

Jake shaded his eyes as it ground to a stop.

Ready or not, here they were. Yeah. Travis getting out from the driver's side, Caleb from the passenger's side…

The General from the rear.

Jacob couldn't believe it. His father? Here? Impossible. Maybe he'd been out in the sun longer than he'd thought. Maybe he was having a hallucination....

"Jacob," his father said.

So much for hallucinations.

What now? Did he salute? No. He was no longer in the service. And salutes didn't go with dirt-smeared jeans and sweaty shirts.

Instead, he stepped forward and stuck out his hand. It was dirt-smeared, too. His father looked at it. Then he took it in his.

"I'm happy to see you, son."

Jake nodded. "It's good to see you, too, sir."

His brothers stopped just behind the General.

"Jake," they said.

Heads nodded. Hands were shaken. And then Jake thought, *Enough,* and cleared his throat.

"So, the three of you just happened to be in the neighborhood and you figured you'd drop by?"

Caleb and Travis almost smiled. The General scowled.

"We made this trip specifically to see you, Jacob."

So much for attempts, however pathetic, at humor.

And that "Jacob" thing…

How come, when Addison had called him "Jacob" it had sounded so soft and loving, not like a—a cold commentary, which was how it sounded, on his father's lips?

"May we sit?"

Jake looked around. The house was out of the question. He'd started work on it a couple of weeks ago, before he'd made the purchase official, and he'd pretty much emptied all the furniture from the rooms on the first floor.

"Ah, sure," he said. "The porch is shady, and there's a six-pack of beer in that old cooler in the corner."

The General marched up the steps. Did he ever walk? Not that Jake could remember. His brothers followed. The General took a chair. So did his brothers.

Bees droned in the eaves.

Nobody reached for the beer, except Jake.

Caleb and Travis followed suit.

Then, amazingly enough, so did the General.

All three Wilde brothers stared at him. Had any of them ever seen him drink beer before?

Jake considered offering to get him a glass.

Then he thought, *To hell with that,* opened the longneck, tilted back his head and took a long, cold drink.

So did his brothers.

His father just sat there with the bottle in his hand.

"Okay, gentlemen. You want to tell me why you're here?"

The General didn't answer. Caleb and Travis looked at each other. Then Travis leaned forward.

"Where have you been?"

"Here and there."

"That's very illuminating."

"I did some traveling. Is that more illuminating?"

"Why didn't you get in touch with us?"

"I did. I sent—"

"That useless message. Yeah. We know. Would it have killed you to have called?"

The muscle in Jake's cheek danced.

"I don't know," he said softly. "There are times I thought it might have."

"What in hell does that mean?"

"It means I needed time to think. Just think, you know? Me, myself and I." Jake's expression softened. "I'm sorry if I worried you guys. That was the last thing I intended."

"And maybe you think it was okay, too, not telling us if you were alive."

"I did tell you." Jake finished his beer, put the bottle on the floor beside him. "I texted."

"'Do not worry about me,'" Caleb growled.

"'I am fine,'" Travis added. His mouth twisted. "Very illuminating."

"It sounded like it was sent by a robot. Anybody ever tell you people speak in contractions?"

Jake raised one eyebrow. "So, I should have said, 'Don't worry about me? I'm fine,' instead of what I did say?"

Caleb opened his mouth, then clamped it shut. Travis made a sound that was suspiciously like a snort of laughter and Caleb shot him a look.

Jake took pity on them both.

"I didn't call or write because I wasn't ready to call or write," he said quietly.

"Even about buying this place?"

Jake shrugged. "I knew you'd hear about it."

"And?"

"And, what?"

His brothers exchanged a look.

"Jake," Travis said gently, "you can't go on like this."

"Hating the world, hating yourself." Caleb shook his head. "And for no reason, man. No reason that's valid."

Jake nodded. "Well, the reason was valid. For me, anyway. What it might not have been was logical."

"Exact—" Travis frowned. "What did you say?"

"I said…" Jake shook his head. "It's complicated."

His brothers looked bewildered. Jake couldn't blame them. Until recently, he'd been bewildered, too, except that was too polite a way to describe it.

"Post-traumatic stress," he said quietly. "It hit me, hard. Guilt over what I'd done and hadn't done—"

"You did all you could."

"I'm still working through that, Trav. I don't know what would have happened if I'd threatened to beat the crap out of my commanding officer sooner—"

"What? You never told us—"

The General cleared his throat.

Until that moment, his sons had pretty much forgotten he was there. Now, he, too, rose from his seat.

"That was wrong, Jacob. Very wrong. It deserved court-martial."

"Yes, sir, it did."

"A soldier obeys orders."

"Yes, sir. I know that."

"There was no excuse for your behavior."

"No, sir. No excuse." Jake's jaw tightened. "But there sure as hell was a damn good reason."

A tight, barely discernible smile came and went on the General's lips. He put his untouched longneck aside, reached out and squeezed Jake's arm.

"Some might agree with that assessment," he said softly. "You've made progress, son."

"Thank you, sir. But I haven't done it alone. I've been attending a veteran's support group."

"Excellent. Excellent. For a while there, I was, well, I was concerned you'd lost your way."

"I had. For a while." Jake swallowed hard. "But someone came along and—and pointed me in the right direction."

"Addison," Travis said softly.

The General nodded. "Addison McDowell."

"How did you—"

"You're my son, Jacob. Did you think I

wouldn't be interested in what was happening to you?" He paused. "She sounds like quite a young woman."

"Yes. She is."

"You opened up to her?"

Jake nodded.

"I'm glad. That you could do that. With her, if not with…" The General cleared his throat. "Well," he said briskly, "I have to get back to D.C. I'm having dinner with the vice president."

Jake and his brothers stood up, too. Caleb clapped his hand on Jake's shoulder. "So, things are good?"

"Yeah. They are."

Caleb and Travis exchanged glances.

"What?" Jake said.

Travis looked uncomfortable. "Ah, she called. Addison. She, ah, she fired us both."

Jake gave a rueful laugh. "Sorry about that."

"No, it was okay. She just said she, ah, she wouldn't need our services any—"

"The thing is," Caleb interrupted, "she asked about you. Wanted to know if you were okay."

Everything seemed to go very still. Jake stared at his brothers.

"Did she—did she—"

Travis squeezed Jake's shoulder.

Travis shook his head. "Sorry, man."

For a long moment, no one spoke. Then Caleb gestured around them. "You bought this place because of her."

"She'd come to love it. That was what she said, anyway." Jake cleared his throat. "Besides, how could I let that miserable old man's land be bought by somebody who might have been even more miserable?"

They all managed to smile.

"Right," the General said. "I only wish you wanted to—"

"But I do," Jake said. He looked at father. "I was wrong about *El Sueño.* And I'd be honored if you offered it to me again."

His brothers grinned. The General smiled. And saluted his son.

"The honor would be mine," he said quietly.

Jake returned his father's salute. The men's gazes met and then the General's mouth twisted. He closed the distance between them and put his arms around his son.

Jake stood, unmoving. His vision blurred. Pollen. It had to be pollen….

He gave a soft, choked sound.

"Dad," he whispered, and he returned the embrace.

In late afternoon, Jake sat in one of the old chairs on his porch, feet up on the railing, a cold bottle of beer in his hand.

A chipmunk came scurrying around the corner.

Jake raised his beer in greeting.

"Welcome," he said amiably.

The chipmunk looked at him.

"Want a beer?"

Evidently not. Potato-chip crumbs from Jake's al fresco lunch hours before were its snack of choice, maybe a bit of the cheese sandwich that had accompanied the chips....

A cheese sandwich.

Jake got to his feet. The chipmunk squeaked in alarm and raced down the steps. Foolish, because it had nothing to fear.

He was the one who was afraid. What he was thinking was crazy.

Addison wouldn't want to see him.

She had a tender heart. That was why she'd asked about him but why would she want to see him after the things he'd said?

Still, if there was a chance…

Even if there wasn't, he needed to see her. To tell her that whatever was happening to him now, he owed to her.

It had taken him a long time to face reality. To admit he needed help. To phone the shrink back at Walter Reed and ask him for the name of a local veteran's group.

But he'd done it.

He'd taken a seat in a circle made up of men just like him, warriors who had served their nation and come home to a world they didn't understand.

If he could do that…

Surely, he could do this, too.

Jake took a deep breath.

Then he went into the house and packed a bag.

CHAPTER THIRTEEN

ADDISON was almost finished packing up her office.

Just a couple more drawers to empty and she'd be done.

Actually, there hadn't been all that much to pack.

A couple of pens. A notebook she'd promised herself she'd use as a diary but never had. A photo of her father and her mother, she a smiling toddler in her father's arms. A photo of Charlie, and one of herself at her law school graduation.

A photo of the Chambers ranch.

That was how she thought of it.

Charlie hadn't owned the place long enough for her to be able to connect his name to those endless acres.

She hadn't, either.

Only a crotchety old man had left his mark

on the place. Pretty sad, when she thought about it.

Addison sighed, shut the middle drawer of her desk and opened the bottom one.

Maybe the new owner would hang on to the land long enough to make it truly his. Or hers. She had no idea who'd bought it; why would it matter? Just because she was foolish enough to have felt a whisper of sentiment when the Realtor phoned to say they had a buyer…

Sentiment over what? She'd only lived on the ranch for a few weeks, put her own imprint on one room….

Shared that room with Jacob, with Jacob, oh, God, would she ever stop remembering...?

"Ms. McDowell?"

Addison swung around. One of the clerks from HR stood in the open doorway, a professional smile on her face.

"Will you be done soon, Ms. McDowell? I'm sorry to bother you but we have some papers for you to sign."

More papers. Addison tried not to roll her eyes. It seemed as if she'd been signing stuff for days, ever since she'd come awake one morning and realized she needed to change her life.

"Five more minutes," she said brightly. "I'll stop by at HR on my way out."

"Oh, that's not necessary. I have the papers with me. And I'll escort you out."

Addison raised an eyebrow. The clerk had the good grace to blush.

"Just to help you with your things," she said.

A lie, and they both knew it. Addison had quit; she hadn't been fired—"terminated," would have been Human Resources' way of putting it—but Kalich, Kalich and Kalich was still worried she might abscond with company information.

All she wanted to abscond with was herself.

A long time ago—at least, it seemed a long time ago—Charlie had surprised her by saying that someday, she'd realize she wasn't cut out for corporate life.

She'd laughed.

"You're so wrong," she'd replied. "I've always dreamed of this. A big Manhattan law firm. Important clients. Complex cases—"

"Endless work hours. Ruthless clients. Demanding partners. Lots and lots of money but no chance to spend it. Give it time, my dear, and you'll see I'm right."

"You were right, Charlie," she said softly, as she put his framed photo into her briefcase.

"Sorry? Did you say something, Ms. McDowell?"

Addison looked at the HR person.

"I said," Addison told her politely, "give me those papers so I can sign them and get the hell out of here."

Once she was home, if you could say that of a one-bedroom condo with a nosebleed mortgage, high above a street jammed with more people than existed in all of Wilde's Crossing, she dumped her briefcase on the floor in the foyer, kicked off her shoes and started peeling off her legal-eagle summer-weight wool suit even as she headed for the bedroom.

What was with her today? Thinking about the ranch. The house. The town she never wanted to so much as hear about again…

The man who'd broken her heart.

Addison took a quick shower, pulled her wet hair into a low ponytail, put on a ratty T-shirt she'd had since college and a pair of scruffy cotton sweatpants, and went into the kitchen.

Dinner?

She opened the fridge, peered inside. The usual suspects were there. Yogurt. Lettuce. Some fruit. Cottage cheese. Tofu.

No real food? whispered a teasing male voice inside her head. *Not even the fixings for a fried cheese sandwich?*

She slammed the door shut.

This was ridiculous.

She had not thought about Texas or Jacob Wilde in months.

Okay. In weeks.

She sighed, pulled one of the stools from the stone kitchen counter and sank into it.

"In at least three days," she muttered.

Or maybe two.

The truth was, she couldn't stop thinking about Texas. The foolish little town. The falling-down ranch house.

Jacob.

He was in her head, her dreams, he was with her all the time. And she didn't want him there. She'd put all of that behind her.

They'd spent a few days together. It had been exciting.

But that was all.

She had not loved him.

She'd been drawn to his complexity. His

pain. She'd once found a sad-looking goldfish in a bowl on the stoop outside her very first New York apartment.

She didn't like fish, except broiled. As pets, they left a lot to be desired. Still, when the poor thing was still there an hour later, she'd taken it in.

Would she have turned her back on a man who'd been wounded?

"No," she said aloud, as she stood and went searching for her stash of take-out menus, "I wouldn't."

She did hope he'd gotten help. Found peace of mind. She didn't hate him for the things he'd said, that what they'd shared had been fun, that she'd known he was going to leave.

"Why would I hate him?" she said, as she thumbed through the menus.

He was right.

Fun was what they'd had. It was the only thing they'd had. And yes, she'd known he was moving on but she was, too—

Suddenly, unaccountably, her eyes filled with tears.

"Stupid idiot," she said.

Her, not him.

She had never loved Jacob—and what was

with all this talking-to-herself-out-loud foolishness?

She should be celebrating, not babbling. Heck, this was the first day of her new life.

The money from the sale of the ranch had made it possible for her to walk away from the corporate world, just as Charlie had predicted she would someday do.

She'd find a job at a small law firm in Queens. Or maybe in Brooklyn. Find a garden apartment nearby, with a tiny terrace and a patch of green out back.

Why she'd ever wanted to live in crowded Manhattan was beyond her.

It wouldn't be a place where you felt you could reach up and touch the sky like the ranch or Wilde's Crossing, but—

She gave herself a little shake.

Never mind all that. Who cared about ranches and Wilde's Crossing and—and—

Addison said a truly bad word, plucked the top menu from the stack and called for a pizza.

Delivery would take forty-five minutes, the kid who took the order said.

An hour and a half later, Addison was still waiting.

And not calmly.

She should have stayed with yogurt. Or a poached egg.

Or a fried cheese sandwich, and did people really eat such things? Had Jake been serious? Fried cheese. Fried hot dogs. And, dammit, why was she wasting all this time, thinking about a man who, yes, had problems but, double dammit, couldn't she admit the truth?

She had loved him. Problems and all.

And he had pretended to care for her. To be a good guy. To be the most wonderful guy she'd ever known, someone so rare, so sexy, so tender, so strong, so perfectly wonderful that—

That he had broken her silly, useless heart.

The doorbell rang.

Addison narrowed her eyes.

"About time," she muttered.

She went to the door. Undid the bolt. The chain. The lock. And, in her rage at the pizza place—hell, at Jacob, at herself—in that rage, she did something incredibly dumb.

She flung the door open without looking through the peephole.

"You're two hours late," she snarled….

Except she wasn't snarling at a pimply-faced kid holding a box of veggie supreme with feta cheese in his outstretched hands….

She was snarling at Jake.

Tall. Lean. Hard-bodied in a black T-shirt and faded denim jeans, five-o'clock stubble on his jaw, dusty boots on his feet…

"Jacob?" she said in a whisper.

"Addison," he said, "oh, God, Adoré…"

He opened his arms.

She wanted to throw herself into them.

But he wasn't going to break her heart again. She wouldn't let it happen. She was not a fool, she wasn't going to let him hurt her—

"Adoré. I know I don't deserve a second chance. I know I'm not worthy of you, I know I'm the lowest kind of SOB in the world—"

"You are all that, and more."

"I know. That's what I just said. I'm everything you probably want to call me…but—but—"

"You absolutely are," she said, and then a sob burst from her throat and she hurled herself into his arms.

"Of course you are," she whispered, while the tears coursed down her face. "You're awful and cruel and horrible and—and oh, God, oh, God, Jacob, I missed you!"

Jake's arms tightened around her. Her face

was buried in his shoulder; his hands were in her hair.

The woman he loved was in his arms.

Every polite apology he'd rehearsed during the eighteen-hundred-plus miles between the ranch and New York had blown straight out of his head.

The sight of her, his Adoré, that beautiful, unadorned face; the careless hair, the clothes that said, *I am who I am and I don't care what anybody thinks...*

"Adoré," he said, and he took her face in his hands, bent his head to hers and kissed her.

Had anything ever tasted as sweet as her mouth? Had anything ever filled him with the joy he felt as she rose to him and wound her arms around his neck?

He lifted her off her feet, stepped inside the apartment and kicked the door closed behind him.

"Please," she said, "oh, Jacob, please..."

In a movie, this would have been a moment for a swell of romantic music, a slow, artful undressing of lovers who had been apart.

It was none of that. They had been too long without each other.

They had trouble getting the clothes off each other.

His hands felt big and clumsy.

Hers shook.

His belt almost defeated her.

The drawstring of her sweatpants had the same effect on him.

And when, at last, nothing separated them but warm, supple skin, Jacob took his Adoré in his arms and carried her to the sofa, where they joined their bodies, their hearts, their souls.

Afterward, he held her tightly to him.

She kissed his throat.

"I love you," he whispered. "I loved you from that very first night."

"Why didn't you tell me?" she whispered back. "Why did you leave me?"

The room was chilly with big-city air-conditioning. Jake drew a silk throw from the back of the sofa and wrapped her in it.

"I didn't tell you," he said quietly, "because I didn't deserve you."

Addison balled her fist and punched him not so lightly in the shoulder.

"Jacob Wilde, who are you to decide who deserves me and who doesn't?"

He laughed. She smiled. His laughter faded.

"I was a mess, honey. I needed help. I knew

it but I couldn't bring myself to acknowledge it." He cupped her face, smoothed his thumbs over her lips. "Thank you for making me see the truth."

"I didn't do anything but love you, Jacob. I'll always love you."

"Yeah," he said gruffly. "You'd better."

Her chin lifted.

"Or?"

"Or I'll just have to kidnap you, carry you off to the A and J ranch…"

"The what?"

He cleared his throat.

"The A and J ranch. The place that used to be the Chambers ranch. I bought it. It belongs to us now. You and me."

"You bought…?"

"The deed's in both our names—although we'll have to change that, once you're Mrs. Jacob Wilde."

Addison raised her eyebrows.

"You're awfully sure of yourself, Jacob Wilde."

He gave her that cocky grin she adored.

"I am, indeed, Ms. McDowell. You're going to marry me."

She smiled. "First you have to ask me."

"Addison McDowell." Jake took her hand and kissed it. "Will you be my wife?"

Her expression grew serious. Serious enough to make him nervous.

"Adoré," he said. "I'm not giving you a choice here. You have to marry me or—"

"Or?"

"Or my life will be empty."

She sighed. "Mine would be empty, too," she said softly, and Jake gave her a long, sweet kiss.

Then he sat back a little.

The hard part was yet to come.

"I know we have to work out the details. I mean, I know you love New York and your job, but Dallas is a great city and there are lots of big law firms—"

"I want to live in Wilde's Crossing."

Jake's mouth dropped open. She closed it with a gentle touch of her finger.

"And practice law there. There must be a firm that needs—what?"

"Caleb's been talking about opening a branch office in town. He has a lot of clients in Wilde's Crossing—ranchers, businesspeople—but he's determined to find just the right attorney. So, what do you think? Wilde and Wilde, instead of Kalich, Kalich and Kalich?"

Addison laughed. Jake did, too. And then his laughter faded and he slipped the silk throw from her shoulders.

"I've missed you," he said, cupping her breast. "Missed you so much…"

The doorbell rang. Addison groaned.

"I ordered pizza," she whispered.

Jake stood up, got his wallet out of his jeans, took out a hundred-dollar bill.

"Just leave it," he called out, and slid the bill under the door. Then he scooped Addison into his arms. "Where's the bedroom?"

"Through there." She kissed him, her lips curving against his. "Pizza'll be cold by the time we get to it.".

"I don't know how to tell you this," he said, as he lowered her to the bed, "but I'm a cold-pizza man, myself."

"How about that?" Addison said. "So am I."

Then she smiled and opened her arms to her lover.

And Jake knew that he was, at long last, home.

* * * * *